WAYS
AND
TRUTHS
AND
LIVES

WAYS
AND
TRUTHS
AND
LIVES

MATT EDWARDS

atmosphere press

WAYS

Sunday

James Dall sipped his cup of coffee as the pastor made analogies to the parable of The Sower and the Seed.

"...There are those who come to church every Sunday to receive the goodness of God's word, only to conveniently forget it once they leave these walls. As soon as some means of instant gratification stands in the way of righteousness, the truth is choked out and no longer resonates in one's consciousness..."

James was somewhere in between the seed that fell along the path and the seed that fell among the thorns, but he wasn't quite aware of this fact. James didn't know why he still attended church, but he told himself it had something to do with the coffee. The free coffee.

Sunrise Covenant Presbyterian on Andrus and Clearwater served some of James' favorite coffee. They brewed a shade grown, fair trade coffee that was the product of some missionary work I.O.U. program. It was delicious. They even served it in an actual mug instead of a Styrofoam cup. The only drawback was the powdered creamer. James hated powdered creamer.

Once the sermon was over, they ended with one final song of worship. James and the rest of the congregation stood to read the projected lyrics in unison. James sometimes mouthed the words, but he never actually sang them. He knew he was an imposter and felt it necessary to not intensify that fact.

James shuffled towards the back of the sanctuary, avoiding eye contact and trying to steer clear of any annoying conversation.

"Hey—James," a man said, pausing to read James's name tag. James just stared at him blankly. "I'm David, the associate pastor here at Sunrise. How are you doing this morning?"

"I'm fine. Thank you," James said. *Dude, please just leave me alone*, he thought.

"Do you come here regularly? I can't say that I've seen you here before."

"I've been coming occasionally. I, uh, have been going to a few different places, trying to find a place to fit in, you know?"

"Of course, of course. Well, I hope you feel welcome here. And hey, before I forget, we play basketball on Sunday afternoons down at the high school if you ever want to come."

"Oh, okay."

"Do you like basketball?"

When is this guy going to give it a rest? "Yeah, I like it okay."

"I used to be good back when my knees—"

"Sorry to interrupt, but my friend is waiting for me outside. I got to go. Sorry. Thanks for the invite though. I'll keep it in mind."

"Alright; take care, James."

James lied about the friend being outside, but he only

half lied about keeping the basketball invite in mind. James actually loved playing basketball, but he had learned his lesson about playing with church members and pastors long ago. As a teenager, playing at his mom's old church, he always felt as though his presence was threatening to them because they fouled him so violently. It's as if they were trying to hack the sin out of him, initiating penitence on his behalf.

James pushed open the glass doors to a wave of late May sun, still thawing out from another cold, unpredictable spring. *It's times like these I wish I smoked.* After James lit his "mental cigarette," he stuffed his hands in his pockets and sauntered to his car, still feeling a little wired from the coffee.

James unlocked his apartment to find it flooded with light. He had three windows facing east, all for which he was thankful: one was in the kitchen, one was in the living room, and the last was in his bedroom. James found that his mind worked best in the late mornings, sitting by one of these windows, under the robust stimulation of coffee. His mind was quicker, made connections more rapidly, yet meditatively: all perfect qualities for creative thought.

After slightly closing the living room blinds to soften the light, James set a pen and a pocket sized, moleskin journal on the small wood-stained end table separating his recliner from the window. James checked his cell phone for the time. *11:34, still pretty early for a drink.* James found that drinking coffee always led directly to drinking alcohol. At some point, in almost every day, the stimulant gave way to the depressant; it was just a matter of when. James hung his dress shirt and slacks up in his closet and changed into basketball shorts and a t-shirt. Dressing up for church was important to James, to maintain a respectable image, which he felt deterred skeptics and overzealous evangelists.

Sitting down in his blue gray recliner, James picked up his pen and journal, ignoring the TV remote in his peripheral vision. *No devil box yet. Let's be productive.* James thought of himself as a writer and, in fact, had been writing an opinion column for a small time, local paper for a little over three years now, but he had yet to have any of his creative works published in any significant way. With his thirtieth birthday looming in November, James felt like his early life's ambition of becoming a well-known author had failed. He occasionally worked on a novel he'd started years before about a young man who tries to woo his dream girl by playing her birthdate as his lotto numbers every week. For a long time, James had been stuck on how to avoid making the girl seem like a gold digger when the young man eventually won. When James wasn't trying to brainstorm solutions to this problem, he used his journal for dappling in poetry. James had been writing a lot of poetry lately.

Almost an hour had passed, most of which was spent looking at the foothills, tinted green for the few short weeks before they were burdened by the intense summer heat.

James snapped out of a daydream. *What time is it? Well, guess it's time for a drink.* James got up and prepared himself a glass of Old Fitzgerald bourbon on the rocks. He had received the bottle as a gift from his friend, Cade, who thought that James would appreciate the literary reference. James didn't; in fact, his response was, "You know I've been depressed ever since I read 'Winter Dreams' in high school. A piece of my heart died with Judy Jones' beauty." Cade said, "You're weird, dude."

James filled his glass a little over three fingers full and returned to stand in front of his third story window. People were walking along the quiet residential street that ran adjacent to James's apartment building. Most of them probably headed downtown, just a few short blocks away, to enjoy some shopping or to meet up with friends for lunch. After a few people had passed, James noticed an attractive blonde with her hair pulled back in a ponytail, sporting jeans rolled up to her knees, a white tank top, and sunglasses. James marveled at how she walked, casually toting a straw-colored bag looped around her left arm. The liquor seemed to move within his mind in rhythm with her steps. And as soon as James was able to appreciate this phenomenon, she left the frame from which he viewed her. *Another one got away.*

* * *

When James was eleven or twelve, he would sit in his back yard at night and pray for the neighbor girl to come outside. Their back yards were separated by a wooden fence: James's house sitting slightly higher than the other so that, when he sat on his patio furniture, James could easily view the windows and doors of his neighbor's house. Her name was Hailey, and she was an elementary school tomboy. She was an above average tether ball player, fearlessly played touch football in a dress, and even laughed at boys' crude jokes. While Hailey had the reputation of being one of the "cool" girls, James had always found her rather cute too, but he kept that observation to himself. James wasn't in love with her, in fact, he had crushes on other girls; him sitting outside had more to do with the fact that she was close. James simply analyzed the probabilities and thought it wouldn't be <u>that</u> unlikely for her to walk outside at some point, especially if the weather was nice. However logical, this turned out to be wishful thinking. She never came outside.

In high school, James actually went on a date with Hailey. James had moved into another house, which meant a different school and no more waiting for the neighbor girl at night. They bumped into each other at a high school dance and Hailey gave James her pager number. It was a typical date for seventeen-year-olds: James picked her up, they went to a movie, nothing glamorous. Unlike most girls James knew at the time, talking to Hailey was easy. There weren't awkward pauses, and better yet, she still laughed at his jokes. James even noticed when Hailey casually touched his arm or leaned towards him during the movie's more intense moments. And just like a good Seinfeld episode, he over-analyzed every instance. When it came time to walk her to her front door at the end of the night, James couldn't bring himself to kiss her. He didn't know why exactly, but somehow, being in the moment suffocated him. She simply didn't feel like the answer to the prayer filled nights of his past.

James realized his mistake as he backed his car out of her driveway. "You're such a pussy," he said to himself; it wasn't until years later that he figured he'd probably confused and embarrassed Hailey. She never returned his calls after that night.

* * *

James put on his tan slacks, black dress shirt, and drove to his second job at Un Monde Parfait. Un Monde Parfait was a relatively yuppie bistro in an affluent section of downtown. James waited tables there, which, in many ways, contradicted his personality. James didn't dislike everyone all together, but he found few people's company refreshing. Waiting on people often exposed the worst of their nature, but James tolerated the job because it paid well, he scored free liquor, it was a short drive from his apartment, and, most importantly, Ally worked there.

James watched her, as he did every night, leaning over to wipe a table with a wet towel. He pretended to be confused by a customer's bill on the POS screen to get a longer look at Ally's perfectly toned legs, tippy-toed, reaching for the far edge of the table. Her tan skirt clung tight to the curves of her ass; James' mouth hung agape.

"She *has* a boyfriend," a voice said over James' shoulder.

"I know," James said defensively, snapping his eyes back to the screen.

"Hey, I'm just giving you a hard time. She is hot though, huh?" Eric said, hauling a tray of dirty dishes to the kitchen.

"Yeah, she's incredible. Her legs look like a freak'n tennis player's. Tanned, athletic—"

"Like our very own Anna Kournikova!" Eric smiled at his own association.

"Have you ever seen *The Naked Gun* movies?"

"No, why?"

"Really? Dude, you're missing out. Anyway, I was just thinking of this Leslie Nielson line where he says something like, 'She had the kind of legs you could suck on for a day.' "

"Yeah, and?"

"That's it—you'd be laughing if you'd seen the movie," James said with reassurance.

"I'm sure I would. Well, back to work," Eric said as he meandered back to the kitchen.

"Good talk." *I hate it when people don't get allusions.*

The kitchen closed at 10:00pm, at which time James routinely took a break. Dan, the manager, never showed his face that late on a Sunday, which left all the authority in the hands of the employee with the longest tenure. On most nights that James worked, this employee was none other than Tony Costa, his best friend at Un Monde Parfait. Tony's real name was Antonio Costantini, but most people called him Costa. Apparently there used to be another Tony who worked there, but that was well before James was hired. Tony was a fun-loving bartender who everyone enjoyed, but he had no business managing people, mainly because he was profoundly irresponsible on company time and he hated the idea of being seen as a hypocrite.

"Hey, James; break time!" Tony said.

"Okay," James answered, unlacing his waist apron.

"It's slow as shit tonight anyway."

"You don't have to convince me."

Many of the employees maintained rigorous smoking schedules, including Tony, so the service entrance that gave delivery trucks access to the rear of the bistro became a second home for those on break. Tony and James used milk crates and stacks of empty pallets as chairs to find some solace in between the brick buildings of Un Monde Parfait and Silver Creek, the neighboring art gallery/framing shop.

"You wanna smoke?" Tony said, gesturing towards James with a cigarette in hand.

"Nah, I'm cool."

Tony offered James a cigarette every day, knowing full well that James didn't smoke.

"Alright, Jimmy-No-Smoke." Tony also made the habit of giving people mafia sounding wise-guy names. A warped tribute to his ancestry. "So, I see you have the hots for Ally."

"What are you talking about?"

"I can tell by the way you look at her, man. There's hunger in your eyes. You mean business."

" 'Hunger in your eyes,' where did you get that one?" James said chuckling. "Anyways, is it that obvious? You could tell that by just looking?"

"No, I'm just fucking with you. Eric told me."

"What?"

"Yeah, he said you were practically molesting her from across the room."

"Whatever, dude. It wasn't that bad. Plus, if Eric worked out on the floor, he wouldn't be able to keep his pants on. He would do the 'molesting' right up close and personal."

"Yeah, you gotta love those blondes," Tony said, as if to add some tangential eloquence to the conversation while taking a drag from his cigarette.

"I'm not that into her anyway," James said after a short pause. "She's obviously gorgeous and I'd love the chance to fuck her, but she's probably going to marry that pretty-boy boyfriend of hers. What's his name?"

"Orson?" Tony said scratching his chin inquisitively.

"Fuck you. I'm serious."

"Oh, in that case, it's Bartholomew."

"No, it's Luke—or Cameron—"

"Samsonite!"

"K—Ky, it's Kyle! Kyle's his name."

"Yeah, you should probably memorize the boyfriend's name of the girl you're stalking."

"Are you done with your cigarette?"

"Not quite."

"Why do I even come out here with you?"

"Because I told you to. I'm your boss," Tony said, keeping a straight face.

"Okay, whatever. I'm going back inside," James said, dusting off the back of his khakis with a deep sigh.

"How late are you guys open tonight?"

"On a Sunday, we're technically open until 1:00am, but we usually shut down earlier than that, as soon as it gets slow like this," James answered.

"Can we order one last round?"

"Sure."

"Um, I guess I'll have a Fat Tire," said the man who began the inquiry.

"Okay. For you?" James asked of the man on his left.

"What's good here?"

"Well, it depends on what you like." *How long have you been here? And you're pulling this shit now!* James thought as he tried to take a deep, yet subtle breath. "Do you like a darker beer, light beer, something really hoppy?" James offered, trying to cure the man's indecision.

"I'll just have a Bud Light."

"We can do that." *You Fucker!* "And for you?"

"I'll have a Jameson on the rocks, please," answered the third man.

"That's a drink," James commended the man with a point of the finger. "Those will be right out, fellas. Can I get you anything else?"

"I think we're good," said the Fat Tire drinker.

With an affirming nod, James left to go place the order.

Minutes later, as James was retrieving drinks from the bar, he felt a hand slide across his back. He turned over his right shoulder to find a smiling Ally batting her mascara enhanced lashes. James' stomach sank as if he was on a roller coaster's initial descent.

"Hey, James," she said.

"Whoa, you scared me."

"Oh yeah, I am pretty scary," Ally laughed.

"What's up?"

"I was wondering if you could cover my last table; I'm trying to get out of here and they're just hanging out."

"Okay, yeah; that's no problem."

"Are you sure?" she asked as she brushed back strands of blonde hair that had escaped her side ponytail.

"Yeah, you'd do the same for me."

"Wow! You have a very generous opinion of me. I didn't know you were so optimistic, James."

I love it when she says my name. "Hey, what can I

say?"

"Well, I appreciate it. You're so my best friend right now," she said as she began to put on a scarlet red cardigan. "Ah, these stupid shoes." She leaned down to adjust her black and white flat, which was balanced across her left knee, right hand grasping the bar. James' eyes instantly gravitated towards the opening of Ally's black dress shirt. A sparkling pendant hung in the cleavage of her two shapely breasts.

"I'll remember that," James said as she rose.

"What?"

"That I'm your best friend."

"I said 'right now'. You've got to keep up this gentleman-like behavior."

"I'll do my best," James said with a smile, picking up the tray of drinks.

"Alright, well thanks again. Bye, James. Bye, Tony," she waved and then turned towards the front door, letting her hair fall into lusciously lazy curls as she reached the threshold.

"Bye," James muttered to himself.

"And to think, she's probably going to see her boyfriend," Tony said from behind the bar.

James ignored him and served the three men who were awaiting their drinks. *Man, I feel like playing the lottery.*

Monday

James woke early on Monday morning to make his 9:00am staff meeting at *Idyll*. *Idyll* was an artful and intimate weekly publication that circulated among Arbor Valley's more cultured clientele. It resided in the entry ways of businesses all around town, but usually only sparked the interest of those wanting insight on the local music scene, various community events, or eccentric political commentaries. The paper received almost the entirety of its funding from local advertising; consequently, they offered little in salary to someone in James's position as an Opinion Columnist.

James had little passion for his work at *Idyll*, recognizing the irony of a twenty-nine-year-old, single man giving advice to readers with, on average, far more complex life experiences than he, but found a rather shallow contentment in the steady income he was able to compile between his two jobs. Plus, he figured, or at least hoped, that his tenure at the paper and the bistro were only temporary.

Idyll came out every Wednesday, so the paper ran staff meetings on Thursdays to plan the next week's publication, and again on Mondays to allow editors a chance to go over each writer's drafts. The rest of the weekdays had no strict schedule in which to adhere. In fact, James honestly didn't know how much time he was expected to spend at the office. In his first year, he was there as much as possible, often mirroring his editor's comings and goings; but as time passed and observations were conducted, James came into work less and less. He figured that, when the abuse of this freedom was finally called into question, he would change his behavior and ask his superiors to specify their preferred work hours.

James left his apartment at 8:37am with his thumb drive and a travel mug full of coffee. Luckily, *Idyll* was located only a few blocks southeast of Un Monde Parfait, which was only a few blocks northeast of his apartment, carving the majority of James's life into one small obtuse triangle. James arrived earlier than most and sat waiting at the desk in his cubicle, sketching on a notepad to look busy.

"Good morning, James. How was your weekend?" asked Rob, a local news writer.

"Uh, I worked mostly."

"At the restaurant?"

"Yeah; how was yours?"

"Good. Spent some time with the kids. We got outside. Man, the weather was nice, wasn't it?"

"Yeah, it was beautiful," James answered, having a few other greetings of similar nature before heading into the cramped conference room with more than a dozen other staff members. Lauren Duvall, *Idyll's* publisher, ran all staff meetings, after which, the several sections or departments of the paper dispersed for individual breakout sessions. Lauren was a tall, sturdy man who ambled throughout the office in a sloth-like manner. When he spoke, his eyes were calm but critical behind black framed glasses; his speech was articulate and to the point. Lauren cared fervently about the paper, but he acted as though he didn't want to romanticize the work; therefore, he wasted little time in meetings and left socializing and frivolity to others.

Janet Cander was James's direct superior as Opinion Editor. She resembled a Whole Foods employee with short, salt and peppered hair. On typical days, she sported an earth tone hemp skirt and a canvas tote bag depicting some sort of bird motif. Two other writers also temporarily worked on the opinion section. They were part of a six month internship process, after which one of them would be hired full time and the other would be let go. As of now, one wrote a piece for that given week, while the other acted as proofreader for several sections of the paper. James had solidified his role with his column "Periscope," and was guaranteed publication every week; James assumed that Brian and Tori, the other two writers, quietly resented him for this very reason.

"How's everybody doing this week?" Janet asked as the three writers scooted chairs around her desk. Everyone answered with some version of 'pretty good.' "Okay, let's get started. James, what angle are you trying to play with the education issue?"

"I'm essentially addressing the question of whether it is better to enroll your children in traditional public education or some other alternative, like private schools or charter schools, assuming money isn't an issue."

"What are you finding out?" asked Janet.

"That Superintendent Moon is a jackass," Brian

interjected with a smug pseudo-intellectualism.

"Thanks, Brian." *Now shut the fuck up you fairy!* "Well, I plan to stay completely objective, if possible. I sort of want to make the case for each option and then maybe lean one way in the wrap up with some subtle implication."

"I appreciate your journalistic objectivity, but make sure it's readable," Janet said.

"What do you mean?"

"You have to have some bite to it. Some controversy. A reason to pick it up and read it. In this case, I don't want you to be so nice." After a short pause, Janet said, "Are you finding good resources?"

"Yeah, one of my friends is a teacher; I've done some reading on several school district websites, including those of some individual private schools, and I've been looking up some parallel articles from papers around the nation for some comparison on the issue." *Any other smartass comments, Brian?*

"Okay, what do you have so far?"

"My intro is a little rough; I always go back to that at the end, but I think the bulk of my content is there," James said as he passed Janet his draft and some hard copy notes. James always handed over his notes, knowing they were never read, because he thought it created the appearance of revision, as if he had already toiled over the assignment.

"And what about you, Brian?" Janet began asking, as she moved on to the other two writers. James drifted off and paid little attention to what was said. He spent the next ten or twelve minutes fantasizing about Ally, while trying to avoid getting an erection. If a conversation didn't directly affect him, he wasn't all that interested. James had yet to realize that this philosophy carried more negative consequences in his personal life.

Brian Thomas Holland, as he introduced himself, was the son of some of Janet's closest friends, which drew suspicion from other employees, especially Tori. He could afford being a part-time employee for a small local paper because he was second generation money. He was fresh out of college and had little empathy for the true working class, even though he ironically identified himself as a member of the proletariat. Brian was a hobbit version of Lauren Duvall's doppelganger: short, portly, dark hair, glasses, possessing a rich vocabulary. Brian spoke with an effeminate air he mistook for elegance. James detested him for all the previously mentioned reasons.

Tori Jacobsen dyed her hair different colors and wore excessive eye makeup. At present, her hair was shoulder length and jet black with two pink streaks framing her face. She was twenty-five years old, but looked younger, due to her affinity for punk fashion. She wasn't a 'real' punk mind you. She was one of those twenty-first century punks who reference a time period they weren't a part of and will probably never understand. Her work attire was a little toned down, but her coinciding anti-establishment views, which lacked intellectual honesty, were never as muted. She dropped out of college after the first year and transferred to an art institute in the northwest from where she earned a certificate. James had always thought of her as a small dog that barked a lot, because she made a lot of noise, but never said anything of consequence.

"Alright, I'll have my notes back to you by lunch," Janet said, excusing the three writers.

"Hey, you wanna go for a smoke?" Tori asked as they filed out of Janet's cubby sized office, waiting for Brian to get out of earshot.

"Sure," James answered, caught slightly off guard. *What does she want?*

"Alright, let me just grab my bag." Together, they shuffled out back to their staff parking lot where they sat on a curb that separated the asphalt from a small strip of grass. "I have American Spirits; I hope that's okay."

"Oh, it's okay. I don't smoke."

"Then why did you come out here?" Tori said with one eyebrow up.

"Because you asked me. Plus, I could use a little fresh air; and there's really nothing to do on these mornings until we get our drafts back from Janet."

"True. But I feel a little weird smoking by myself."

"What do you mean? You're a smoker. Don't you smoke by yourself all the time?"

"Yeah, I smoke by myself," Tori said, enunciating the last three syllables. "Now, it kind of feels like I have an audience."

"Well, don't mind me. There's no pressure. I won't critique you," James said. Meanwhile, Tori lit her cigarette and was polite enough to exhale through the far corner of her mouth after each drag. *What's the deal? She usually doesn't give me the time of day,* James thought between glances at Tori. *You know, she's actually not half bad looking if she got a normal hairdo and got rid of some of the eye makeup. Besides her small breasts, her body looks pretty nice, at least from what I can see.* James scanned her outfit: unzipped black hoodie, purple and black tank top, dark blue skinny jeans, and sandals.

"Since you mentioned 'critique', part of why I asked you out here was to see if you could look over some stuff I wrote," she said after pondering whether or not to bring it up.

"Oh." *Is she hitting on me?*

"You don't have to do it. I guess—I just respect your opinion and I thought I'd ask."

"I didn't mean to look disinterested or anything. I just wasn't expecting that from you—or anyone really."

"Oh, I'm sorry. Forget about it," she said, trying to laugh it off.

"No, that's okay. What kind of stuff is it any way?"

"Mostly poetry."

"Are you looking to get it published?"

"I guess. I'm not sure. I just want to take the next step. You know?"

"Well, I'd be happy to look it over for you. Do you have it here, or—?"

"Yeah, I have it."

"Do you just want to email it to me today?"

"Sure, let me go do it right now," Tori said, putting out her cigarette.

"I'll give you my personal email. You know, so we're not mixing business with pleasure."

"Oh, okay," she answered with a giggle as they made their way back inside and towards her desk. "Here, you can write it on this," she said, handing him a set of sticky notes.

"Alright...here you go."

"Thank you."

"Well, I guess I'll go do some work or something," James said, sensing the potential for awkwardness.

"Okay, see you later."

"Yeah," James answered, turning away. *She's no Ally, but—*

Brian stared at James as he passed by his cubicle. James ignored him.

James left the *Idyll* office around 2:30pm, mindful of his usual deadline of 10:00am the next day. Dating back to college, James preferred working from the comfort of his own living room, or a place where he could be alone with his thoughts, his habits, and his rituals. The office was a useful place to conduct research, partly because the internet was much faster than at his apartment, and occasionally the benefits of collaboration overrode James's desire to be absolved from communication with his fellow employees. However, James usually only consulted Janet; her opinion was simply the only one that mattered, not because of its supremacy, but because of the position from which it sat. Today, James exchanged a few more pleasantries with Tori than normal, but nothing else of any significance.

James opened the door to an uncomfortably warm apartment, not yet in the routine of trying to keep it cool throughout the day. He proceeded to set his keys down on the kitchen counter and open the refrigerator door. Besides the wave of cold air, nothing met his fancy. Instead, James scooped ice cubes from the freezer and poured himself a generous glass of bourbon. After which, he closed the blinds, turned on the air conditioning, stripped down to his under shirt, and brought his lap top out to the small kitchen table to continue polishing his draft from there.

Halfway through his drink, James texted his friend Cade. "Hey, call me when you're done with work." Cade was a science teacher at an area high school, and he appreciated James's insistence on punctuating text messages. James paced a bit, rephrasing sentences out loud, and then went back to work.

After James reached a point where he felt he was either finished or unable to make any more progress, he checked the time. *4:35, eh, might as well.* He logged on to his email to take a look at Tori's poetry. While a page was loading, James refilled his empty glass. James downloaded an attachment containing a few dozen poems of varying lengths. James started with the first one, entitled, "Stems":

Stems
fragrant darkness, only the shapes
of soul
full of self-worth and misuse,
long nights and half-truths

a dance of interlaced fingers
skin
beautiful anchors
bringing us down

catatonic self- indulgence
in search of color
square pegs and round holes
friction

cut at the wrists,
but not like you think
pruning of aging flowers
 stems relief

James found himself surprised. *The subject matter and imagery is pretty typical, but it's pretty catchy.* James scrolled through the document to scan other titles, not wanting to read them all now, but interested at least. Then James's phone rang; it was Cade.

"What's up?" answered James.

"Nothing, I just got your message."

"Yeah, it's like 5:00. I thought school got out at 3:00?"

"Well, contrary to popular belief, some teachers actually work hard."

"I guess I should have learned that while conducting my research," James was sarcastically, referring to his brief interview of Cade on the issue.

"Well, I hope your readers are more receptive...all fifteen of 'em."

"Ha, ha. Very funny."

"Hey, did you need anything specific, or did you just want to bullshit?"

"Yeah, I was wondering if you wanted to come over tonight and have a few beers or something."

"On a Monday?"

"Hell yeah; Mondays are like my Fridays, or maybe more of a Thursday, but I just felt like doing something, and I thought you might read my final draft before I submit it tomorrow."

"Okay; I'll have to check with the wife, but I'm pretty

sure I can make it over."

"You sure you'll get permission?"

"Yeah, we spent a lot of time together this weekend. She probably wants a break."

"Awesome. What time can you get over here?"

"I don't know. Seven? Do you need me to bring anything?"

"Yeah, some beer you wanna drink."

"Anything else?"

"Nope, I think we're good."

"Alright, I'll see you later."

"Okay, bye."

James put his phone back in his pocket and finished his second drink. He stood for a few minutes in front of his living room window, sucking on the bourbon flavored ice cubes. *How should we kill the next few hours?* James wandered back to his computer and stared at the screen momentarily before sitting down. He closed Tori's document, logged out of his email, and began searching for free porn videos that featured blondes. After half an hour, James went to his bathroom to masturbate and then resigned to watching TV until Cade arrived.

Cade knocked on James' apartment door at 7:10pm holding a six-pack of Lagunitas IPA.

"What's up, dude? Come on in. You can just put that in the fridge."

"Will do. You want one now?"

"Yeah, I'll take one."

Cade opened two bottles with his key chain opener and set the rest in the refrigerator. "Have you had this before?" asked Cade.

"Yeah, it's pretty damn good. We used to have it on tap at my work."

"Speaking of that, my wife and I have meant to come down for dinner some night," Cade said as they made their way into the living room.

"You guys should; the food is great. The service is shitty, though," James said with a smile as he made himself comfortable in his recliner, Cade on the couch along the opposite wall.

"That's what I've heard. So, how's your column going? It's due tomorrow, right?"

"I think it's pretty good. You can tell me whether or not I have command of the issues. I'm trying not to be too cynical, but I've got to have some edge to it; otherwise, I'm stuck with a comprehensive approach, and that's not wise with a thousand word limit."

"Are you trying to picture being a parent facing this decision or what?"

"No," James said with a chuckle. "I try to avoid such things."

"What? Being a parent or seeing things from other people's perspectives?"

"Don't worry. I've looked at the neighborhood from Boo Radley's porch. But to answer your question, parenting is something I simply don't want to think about. And to answer your first question, I'm thinking in terms of a customer more than anything else."

"Aren't parents the true customers?"

"And every taxpayer."

"By the way, I'm a science teacher. Don't try to impress me with your literary references."

"I thought that's why you came over here, to bask in

all my glory." *At least _he_ got it.*

"Yeah, something like that. Just drink your beer."

"Thanks, by the way," James said, lifting his beer in a toasting motion. "Did you eat already?"

"Yeah."

"Well, I'm gonna put a pizza in the oven. You can change the channel if you want," James said, passing the remote like a baton.

Cade was James's age but married with one daughter and another child on the way. He viewed hanging out with James as a reprieve, not because he was unhappy at home, but simply because he was outnumbered, and it felt good to escape estrogen's grasp for a few hours.

"So, I think this girl at the paper was hitting on me today," James said from the kitchen, knowing no way to transition to the subject cunningly.

"Oh yeah? Who?"

"Just some girl. She works on the opinion section too. She sort of shares a role with this other guy."

"Has she worked there long?"

"No, she just started this year."

"So, is she cute or what?"

"That's just the thing. She's kind of got this punk look going, which is inherently dreadful, but there's some weird quality about her that's alluring."

"I'm assuming you just noticed this quality today, right?"

"Yeah, I guess so."

"You just like her because you think she likes you. That's the mysterious allure," Cade said, pointing as if he'd just identified the smoking gun. "It happens to high schoolers all the time."

"You know, she probably looks like one of your students," James said in an effort to deflect Cade's assertion. "I thought she was eighteen when she started working there."

"How old is she?"

"Twenty-three, I think."

"Are you gonna go out with her or what?"

"I don't know. I'll probably just let things play out a little bit. Maybe—" James said as he sat back down.

"What about Amber?"

"What about her?"

"I thought you two were sort of an item."

"Who told you that?" James said defensively.

"She hinted at it I guess, but mostly I thought it was implied."

"Why?"

"Because you guys spend time together, you've known each other for a while, and you've had sex with her, right?"

"Yeah, so what?"

"Well, I think she may be under the impression that you guys are a little more serious than you're making it out to be."

"For your information, I haven't talked to her in a couple of weeks."

"Really? What happened?"

"Nothing really. I just haven't talked to her."

"Why not?"

"I don't know. I guess she just doesn't really do it for me. You know? If someone doesn't just make you go 'wow', you probably shouldn't be with them." *I'd bring up Ally, but—*

"I guess so. I just thought she'd be good for you."

"Why?"

"She's kind of cute, and she's nice. She's just a nice girl," Cade said, shrugging his shoulders.

"That's the problem right there. No one wants to be with someone who's nice. If the best thing you can say about a person is that they're nice, then that person is fucked."

"Okay, okay, okay. If that's how you feel, fine. Just make sure you let her know. You know my wife and her are pretty close."

"Don't worry about it. You want another beer?"

"Yeah, I'll have another."

*   *   *

James met Amber almost a year prior on a double date with Cade and his wife, Tara. Tara was friends with Amber and naturally thought the two would make the perfect match. James wasn't initially drawn to Amber, but he continued to go on friendly dates with her because, as he thought at the time, *I don't have anything else going for me.* What James didn't admit, not even to himself, was that he craved the positivity and warmth of Amber's temperament. Amber possessed an innately gentle spirit and she showered James with compliments. She was fascinated by his work as a writer, even though he tried to act modest and self-deprecating. Amber was one of the only women, besides his mother, that unashamedly described him as handsome, which embarrassed James, yet steadily inflated his ego, just as it had when his mother did so throughout his adolescence.

By the end of that summer, James and Amber became romantically involved, and not long after, had sex. Weeks later, Amber confessed to James that he was only the second guy she had ever slept with. James panicked.

In an effort to eradicate his own anxiety, James sat Amber down and explained "that I think we're moving a little bit too fast. I like what we have going here; I just don't want to do anything to screw it up, and I feel like that's happened in the past. Does that make sense?" Amber answered, "Yeah, I think so...I do appreciate you sharing your thoughts, though. Most guys try to hide what they're feeling." James was pleased with her response. Amber had mixed feelings, but in the quietness of her own thoughts she mistakenly took James's concerns as a form of com-mitment. She felt that if he was willing to maintain the relationship and slow things down romantically, then he must respect her more than others he had dated. She truly saw James in too good of a light.

James effectively strung Amber along for several months as their dates became less and less frequent. By the New Year, it was clear to both James and Amber that their relationship, in any romantic sense, had died. Amber's non-confrontational manner allowed their situation to wither away naturally, including James's faint whisper of guilt.

In late March, Cade threw a Spring Break/birthday party for his wife. James and Amber silently agreed that they didn't want one of their absences to create any awkward tension or inquiries from the hosts, so they both attended. For the most part they politely avoided each other, but James was determined to at least say hello and make small talk, which was his subtle way of apologizing.

By midnight, twenty or more house guests flooded the living room to dance, enticed by their confidence-rich drink of choice. James found himself in one corner trying to guard his drink from overzealous couples, when he spotted Amber from across the room. Once her eyes found his, James smiled and Amber raised her glass of wine in recognition. By the end of the party, Amber was too drunk to drive. When she asked James to take her home, he consented. When she invited James inside, he accepted. They had sex on her couch; when Amber woke up, James was already gone.

Tuesday

James woke up with a dull canopy of a headache. In front of the bathroom mirror, he rubbed temples, inspected bloodshot eyes, and ran his fingers through dark brown, disheveled hair. *Bourbon followed by IPA isn't always a great idea...It's not that bad. We look fine.*

James arrived at the *Idyll* office a little after 9:00am, wanting to reread his final draft before submitting it. His morning was uneventful. After having a brief conversation with Janet, James spent time sifting through *Idyll's* email suggestion box. To keep material relevant to their readers' interests, *Idyll* tried to respond directly to local questions and concerns, especially in the opinion section. James resented getting his ideas straight from these people with too much time on their hands, but it was necessary and clearly useful.

By lunch time, James was ready to go home, but he had yet to receive any word from Janet concerning his piece. She was usually very punctual, making final cuts and edits by noon each Tuesday. On his way out to grab a sandwich, James stopped by Janet's office to inquire about the delay. He knocked lightly on the door.

"Come on in—oh, hey, James."

"Hi, I was just heading out for some food and I was wondering if you were done with my draft."

"Oh, sorry. I've been done with it for a while. I handed it to Tori for proofreading."

"Oh, okay. What did you think?"

"I think it is really interesting. I'm glad to see you took my advice from yesterday."

"So, it's good?" James asked with a thumbs-up.

"Yeah, I just made a few adjustments to tighten up a couple sentences. If you want, Tori's probably still going over it; you can check out what I changed and make sure you're okay with it."

Sounds like a good excuse to talk to her. "Alright, thanks."

"See you after lunch."

"Yep, see you," James said as he headed back towards the cubicles.

Tori was proofreading the opinion section, and a few others, because it was Brian's week to be published. These were the types of details that escaped James' attention span.

"Hey, Tori, how's it goin'?"

"It's goin'."

"You don't seem too excited about it."

"Would you be?"

"No, probably not." *Sorry I asked.* "Are they that bad?"

"No, it's not that. It just gets so tedious. But yours is good," Tori said, realizing what James may have implied.

"Oh, thanks. You think so?"

"Yeah, I've never thought about it like that before. It'll

make people think."

"It will probably piss a lot of people off."

"But isn't that the point?" she said with a shrug and a mischievous smile.

"It is as long as I keep my job."

"Well, at least you get to write every week. I'm stuck here doing this."

"Hey, I read one of your poems."

"Oh, yeah? Just one?"

"Well, I was still working on my column last night and I didn't have a bunch of time. But I'll read the rest soon. Don't worry."

"No worries. I was just messing with you," she said as she spun towards him in her chair.

James's eyes scanned past Tori's Ramones t-shirt to catch a glimpse of her pale, thin legs reaching out from a black pleated skirt. "Okay, good. I don't want to get on your bad side."

"Who says you already aren't?"

"Well then, I better mind my manners and let you get back to work."

"If you must."

"I was just going out for a sandwich; do you want anything?"

"No, thank you."

"Alright, I'll talk to you later," James said as he turned to leave.

"Hey, wait," Tori called, causing him to spin around. "Would you like to go to a show Thursday night?"

"Who's playing?"

"Some punk bands you've probably never heard of."

"So, not the Ramones?" James said, pointing to her

shirt.

"No. Not quite," she laughed. "You in?"

"Yeah, I'm in," James said, without hesitation.

"Good. When you come back from lunch, I'll give you more details."

"Okay, I'll see you in a bit. Thanks for the invite."

"You are very welcome."

She's like a completely different person.

Wednesday

James left work early and was home by 2:44pm. Soon, he found himself in front of his computer watching a video of a busty blonde showering with a petite brunette with an upper arm tattoo. They were supposedly two dedicated cheerleaders making use of the only working shower head after a late-night practice in preparation for the state competition. *The premise is everything.*

Just as the brunette was lathering up the blonde's very prominent breasts, James's phone rang. It was his mother.

"Hello," James answered after muting but not pausing the video.

"Oh, hi. I didn't expect you to answer."

"Yeah, I came home early today. Tryin' to get some work done."

"Well, I won't keep you long. I just wanted to ask you a quick question."

"Okay."

The two cheerleaders started kissing softly, frequently giggling in their attempts to fake embarrassment.

"Well, I was wonderin'—actually, Gene and I were

wondering if you would like to be involved in Trisha's wedding. She is your sister after all."

"First of all, she's not my sister, mom. She's my stepsister. And she's not even that. I've met her twice."

"That reminds me. You never come and visit."

The brunette began sucking on the blonde's breasts as the blonde fingered herself.

"Me?" You're the one who got married to what's-his-face the same week I graduated college and moved to Ashland two months later."

"His name is Gene, James. And he is your stepfather."

"You can call him whatever you want, but he's just Gene to me and nothing else."

"What has he done to offend you?"

"Nothing. He hasn't done anything. I don't have a problem with him. You just can't expect me to have an affinity for someone just because you're married to him."

"You know, he's tried really hard to be sensitive to your situation."

"And what situation is that?"

"You know."

"No, I don't think I do."

"You know, growing up without a father. Living by yourself with no family around. That sort of thing."

By now, the brunette was licking the blonde from behind while the blonde clutched the center column of shower heads, writhing her head back in exaggerated ecstasy.

"Tell Gene that I appreciate his sympathy, but he can save his sensitivity for his own daughters."

James's mother hesitated before responding. "So, does that mean you don't want to be a part of the wedding?"

"Yes."

"Will you at least come? To see me if nothing else."

"When is it?"

"August 28th."

"I'll see."

"Ah, come on. Let me see that handsome face."

"There you go again."

"What? A mother can't compliment her son?"

"No, you can." James paused the video before the blonde could return the favor. "It's just that—"

"What?"

"I haven't heard that for a while."

"Aw, James. You need to get out more. Some lucky lady is just sitting out there waiting for you."

"I wish that were true."

"You'd be surprised."

"I'll keep that in mind. I will."

"I hope that you do."

"Alright, mom. I've got to get back to work. I'll let you know about the wedding soon."

"Okay, James. I love you."

"Love you too. Goodbye."

Thursday

James parked his car a little over two blocks from The Encore, which sat on the west edge of downtown, between Columbia Avenue and Steunenberg Street. As he turned from Columbia and into the alley leading to the main entrance, he immediately spotted Tori standing in a small circle of friends corralled in a designated smoking area. When Tori noticed James, she waved him over to the group.

"Hi, there," Tori said.

"Hey, how's it goin'?"

"Swell. You wanna meet my friends?"

"Sure," James answered, smiling awkwardly at the expressionless faces. James extended a hand that was eventually met by an assortment of frail limbs hanging from loose fitting tank tops and black Avenged Sevenfold t-shirts, cutoff shorts and shredded jeans, limp mohawks and veils of bangs.

"Nice to meet you guys," James concluded, imagining what they must think of his non-descript clothing of jeans and a black polo. Very un-punk. *They all look so young.*

"We were just talking about how Establishment Zero is trying to sound just like old Anti-Flag stuff," Tori said.

"No, they're more of a Pennywise knock off," a face-full-of-bangs interjected.

"Do you know any of those bands?" asked Tori.

"I know who Anti-Flag and Pennywise are, but I've never really listened to them," James said.

"What kind of music do you like?" asked the talking limp mohawk.

"60's and 70's rock mostly; 90's grunge and some other stuff. Anything but rap and country really."

"Are you guys done with your cigarettes? I'm ready to go inside," Tori said as she put hers out under her white flats adorned with little black, clearly hand drawn, musical notes.

"Nice shoes!" James remarked.

"Thanks. They're my dancing shoes. You guys ready?"

James followed Tori to the line of people waiting to get in, his eyes glued to her petite frame swaying within blue skinny jeans and a tight red t-shirt. They paid their cover charge, received their wristbands, and descended a staircase to their left which led them to the bar area.

"Do you want a drink?" Tori asked James. "I think we have a while before the first band starts."

"Yeah, I could go for one."

James ordered a whiskey sour, Tori ordered a vodka tonic, and Tori's friends all ordered Pabst Blue Ribbon. After receiving their drinks, they huddled off to the side of the bar and exchanged anecdotes about people James didn't know. With nothing to say, James steadily sipped his drink and tried to look interested. After fifteen or twenty minutes of waiting, the first band stepped on stage, introduced themselves as Kick Back, and began with a quick firing bass drum and a mêlée of high-pitched power chords. When the first song ended, Tori leaned into James and said, "We're going down to the floor, are you coming?"

"No, thanks. I'm alright."

"Come on, it'll be fun."

"Maybe later."

"Okay, but you're missing out," Tori said before slamming the rest of her drink.

"I'll be at the bar—" James began, but then realized it was no use; she already started towards the floor and the second song was at full volume. *Alright, I'll just sit and drink and listen to music I don't really like.* "I'll have another whiskey sour," James said, positioning himself on a bar stool. *The only way to make well whiskey tolerable.*

James watched the dance floor over his left shoulder. However early, the floor was more than half full of participants dressed in a mosaic of denim and black and metal and multi-colored hair. Tori was easy to spot in her red shirt, jumping maniacally, hair resembling a cheer leader's pom-pom. Other people caught James's eye as well. On the far edge of the floor a young couple, probably with fake IDs, made out during most of every song. *No one wants to see that.* James was also struck by a few small pockets of older people in the crowd. Not far from where he sat, gray haired men in leather jackets bobbed their heads, careful not to spill their beer. *Sweet! I thought I was the oldest one here.* After several songs, which seemed like mere alterations of the first one, James affirmed his dislike for punk music. *I don't know how much longer I can stay.*

James finished his second drink as Tori ascended the short steps separating the floor from the bar area. Tori was joined by a rather obese friend who draped her curves in an unfortunate mish mash of all black.

"Hey, James, this is my friend, Clover."

"Hey, how's it goin'?" James asked as he shook her clammy hand.

"She has something for me in her car. We'll be right back, okay," Tori said with a hand on James's shoulder.

"Okay," James said, spinning in his bar stool to watch them leave.

The first band ended and people from the floor started to flood the bar area. James found himself leaning to one side or the other as people wedged themselves in position to order from the bartender. James tapped his foot on the bar stool anxiously, hoping Tori would re-emerge soon.

Finally, James saw Tori and Clover coming down the stairs. James turned back to the bar to appear as if he wasn't waiting. Most of the crowd had walked back down to the floor.

"Hey, we're back," Tori said, sliding into the seat on James's left. She reeked of smoke and cheap vanilla perfume.

"Did you lose Clover?" James asked.

"No, she went to go mingle with some of her other friends. Man, I need a drink," she said, gesturing towards the bartender. "Do you need another one?"

"Yeah, why not?"

"So, how did you like the first band?"

"They weren't bad," James said, maintaining some politeness. "They definitely had a lot of energy."

"Cool. This next band is supposed to be alright, I haven't heard all their stuff, but the band after them fucking rocks."

"What's their name?"

"FIGHT. It's an acronym. It stands for Freedom Is Gone Holy Terror," Tori said, sensing James' need for clarification.

"Interesting. Very subtle," James responded with a smirk.

"Can I get you guys something?" the bartender interjected.

"I'll have a vodka tonic," Tori answered without hesitation.

"Do you guys have Jameson?"

"Unfortunately not. All I've got is Jim Beam."

"Alright, I'll have a glass of that on the rocks, please."

"Okay."

"Make it a double," James added.

"You got it."

"Wow, look at you. You're getting serious now aren't you?" Tori said.

"What can I say?"

"I'm impressed."

"Well, I was impressed with your dance moves."

"Oh yeah, you were watching? Well, you haven't seen nothin' yet."

"Here you guys go," the bartender said, placing the drinks in front them.

"Just put it on my tab," James said.

"You bet."

"Thank you," Tori said to James.

"No problem."

As they reached for their drinks, Tori leaned over and whispered, "Hey, do you want one?" She extended her tongue momentarily, revealing a small white pill.

"What is it?" James asked.

"Call it a 'pick me up'."

"I think I'm good."

"Alright, just thought I'd ask."

They each sipped their drink as the second band began to play.

Once the music began, conversation was useless. As in every case, James and Tori tried to yell over the music, but soon grew weary from their efforts. After a few songs, Tori rejoined her friends on the floor. James decided to stretch his legs and watch the second act from the railing that separated the upper bar area from the dance floor. James enjoyed the second band a bit more. They possessed a more mature sound, including varied chord progressions and well orchestrated build ups. James was no musical expert, but the difference in skill and experience was palpable.

In between sips, James surveyed Tori and her friends, a little suspicious of the drugs they were on. *This girl is crazy. Speaking of which,* James thought as he inspected his own glass, *I better slow down.*

As the second band concluded, James found a sweaty version of Tori, and followed her and her friends outside for a smoke break. After minutes of being more of an observer than a participant, James excused himself.

"I'm gonna run and use the bathroom before this last band starts to play," James said to Tori in an aside. "I'll meet you inside."

"Okay, we're almost done."

James snaked his way around the far side of the bar

to a hallway on the opposite end of the facility. James waited in line for the urinal as someone impatiently brushed past him and proceeded to pee in the sink. *I guess it's just that kind of place.* After James finished his business, he wandered back towards the bar to find Tori lining up a row of shot glasses.

"What's all this?" James asked, taking a seat.

"You're gonna do a shot with me," Tori answered.

"What is it?"

"You'll just have to drink and find out," she said, scooting the clear liquid towards him. James lifted the shot glass to his nose. *Smells like tequila.* "Here you go," Tori said as she distributed shots to the friends standing behind her. "You ready, James?"

"As ready as—"

"Good! Here we go everybody," Tori lifted her glass as her friends reciprocated. "Whooo," she cheered as she tilted back her head.

"Oh man!"

"I love it! You want another one?" Tori said with an ecstatic grin, placing her hand on James' thigh.

"I don't know. I kind of want to let this one hit me first."

"You're probably right. Well, while you're thinking about it, I'm going to do something about this sweaty mess. Talk about out of control," Tori said, almost singing the last part. She then pulled the majority of her hair into a pony tail, leaving only her pink streaks. Just as she finished, the house lights went black and the crowd roared as the final band took the stage. "Oh my god, there they are!"

"Oh, cool."

"Come on! You don't have a choice. You've got to dance with me," Tori said, springing from her seat.

"Okay," James answered submissively. As soon as James's feet touched the ground, his head filled with an intense swarm. *Oh shit.* With his peripheral vision slightly blurred, he focused only on Tori's red shirt and the thin hand pulling him to the dance floor. He instantly hit a humid mass of humanity.

James couldn't quite react to the music itself, but instead tried to keep up with Tori's pace. As she jumped to the beat of the song, arms flailing, head shaking; James could only mimic one motion at a time, leaving him horribly out of sync. James could feel the guitar and the bass and the drums pulsating through his chest, but his response time was drowning in a confusing mix of Jim Beam and José Cuervo.

In between the first and second song, Tori fanned herself with both hands and then rolled her shirt up to just below her breasts. "God I'm hot, but you guys fucking rock!" she yelled as James's eyes locked onto her bare lower back. The guitars initiated the second song and James crept closer to Tori as people started to push towards the front. He could feel her warmth as she turned back to him with a smile. As she danced, James could feel Tori moving back into him, as if pushed by the raucous crowd. Purely for stability, James placed his hands on her hips as they jostled about. Immediately, she responded by grasping his hands and moving them slowly up the front of her body. He felt the beads of sweat on her flat stomach as his palms inched towards her breasts. Once there, she arched her back into him, eliminating all space between their bodies.

As the song ended, she released her grasp to applaud the band members. As soon as the applause subsided, Tori reached for James's hand and headed to the opposite end of the dance floor. She led him off the floor, back towards the bar, and then took a sharp left at the hallway leading to the bathrooms. As soon as she rounded the corner, she turned and pulled James into her, almost clumsily. With her back against the wall, she reached up with both hands and held James's face as she leaned forward to kiss him. He responded by placing his hands on her back, pulling her body into his, as their tongues lashed together sloppily. James's mouth was too numb to taste the lingering cigarettes.

"Hey, what are you guys doing?" a member of security barked. "You can't do that here. Go on. Move it."

What would normally be embarrassing felt like more of a nuisance as Tori and James made their way back to the floor.

"Do you want to go somewhere else?" James asked, not sure if she could hear him over the music.

"You've really got to see these guys! They're just getting warmed up."

"Okay." *Should I bring her to my place?*

The dance floor was pure chaos. Tori slithered her way through the crowd, looking for some of her friends. James tried to keep her in view but found people to be less polite to him as he tried to slide between strange bodies. It wasn't long before they were separated by the constant pushing of the crowd. *Fuck! Where'd she go?* James looked for her, standing on his tip toes, fighting to keep his balance. *Ah, screw it! I need to sit down any ways. I'll catch her on the way out.*

James, the only person not in awe of the band on stage, made his way back to the bar where he ordered another whiskey on the rocks and a much needed water. James spent the duration of the show concentrating on the drinks in front of him and calming the storm in his head. While stirring his whiskey, James, aroused by his primal instincts, imagined various scenarios in which he could get Tori to himself that night. However, any scenario that involved too many steps felt overly complicated to his intoxicated frontal lobe and soon dissolved. His 'official plan' resembled the remnants of his whiskey glass when FIGHT said, "thank you" and "good night."

The house lights came up and James swiveled towards the floor. As waves of people exited the floor and scattered towards the exits, James became increasingly nervous. *Alright, where the hell is she?* Just then, James spotted Tori's friends walking his way.

"Hey, uh, guys," James said with a wave of his hand.

"Hey, what's up?" one of them answered.

"Have you guys seen Tori?"

"Ah, no, not for a while."

"I think she left already," another one said.

"You're serious? Like just now?" James asked.

"No, I think she took off with Clover and some other people before the show even ended."

"Do you guys have a way of getting a hold of her?"

"Sorry, man, my phone is dead."

"If we find Chris, he probably has it."

"No, don't worry about it," James said, not wanting to cause them trouble or feel like a creep. "I'll see her at work. Thanks though."

"Hey, no problem. Did you enjoy the show at least?"

"I guess so," James said shrugging his shoulders, having already shifted focus away from the conversation.

"Well, take it easy," one said with a pat on James's shoulder.

"Yeah, you too. See you," James said, turning back to his empty drink, ignorant of their waves goodbye.

*What the fuck's wrong with her? She's probably with some other guy—*James stopped himself. *Why would I be jealous? She's just a crazy pill-popping bitch. Forget it. What time is it?* James pulled out his cell phone to check the time. *It's already after 11:00. Who sent me a message?* It was a text from Amber, sent at 8:37pm.

"I want to see you. Call me."

What the hell?—Man, this night can't get any weirder. "Can I close out my tab?"

James tried to take deep breaths as he walked back to his car, knowing full well that he shouldn't drive. *I'll be fine. I'm going straight home,* he rationalized. James crossed Columbia, phone in hand, pondering whether or not to text Amber back. As a slight, drunken smile emerged on his face, James texted back, "Are you still up?" then he opened his car door and began to drive home.

James felt a vibration in his pocket as he entered his apartment complex's parking garage. Once the car was parked, James checked the message.

"Yeah, sort of. Can you talk?"

James decided to call.

"Hello?"

"What do you mean by 'sort of' up?"

"Well, I'm dressed for bed and all, but I hadn't quite fallen asleep," Amber said in quiet voice.

"Oh, I see," James paused briefly. "Do you want to come over?"

"What time is it?"

"A little after eleven," James said. It was 11:21pm.

"Umm—sure, but only for a little while," Amber said after a deep sigh.

"Okay, cool. I have to work tomorrow too."

"Let me just put something on and I'll be right over."

"Okay, see you soon."

"Bye."

Adorned with a clean shirt and a fresh spray of cologne, James was trying to down a tall glass of water when he heard Amber's knock at the door.

"Just a second," James said, making his way to the door. As he opened it, he found Amber's dark brown, pacifying eyes glance up from the floor to meet his. She was conservatively dressed in jeans and a grey cable-knit sweater. She tucked her shoulder length, tawny hair behind her ear as she formed a smile. "Come on in," he said.

"Thanks. So, what kept you up so late tonight?"

"I was at a concert."

"Oh yeah, who was playing?"

"To tell you the truth, I don't really know. It was a punk show. Some people at work invited me. It wasn't really my thing."

"This was people from *Idyll*?"

"Yeah—please sit down," James interrupted himself, gesturing to the couch with his hand.

"Thanks."

"Do you want something to drink?"

"No thanks. It's late, I'll have to pass."

"Not even some water?"

"No, I'm alright."

"Are you sure?" James asked with a smile.

"Yes, I'm quite sure. Now would you just come over here and sit down?" Amber replied with a nervous smile of her own.

"Yeah, sure," James answered, sitting down close to Amber as she crossed her legs. "What's up? You look like you have something on your mind."

"I do," she said, tapping the arm of the couch with her fingers.

"Well, what is it?" James asked with impatience. "You can tell me," James placed his hand on her thigh as he said this.

"Yeah, I know. You've always been easy to talk to. I just—I—don't know how to say it exactly."

"Take your time." He now began to rub her thigh.

"Stop," Amber said, as she quickly enclosed his hand in both of hers, removing it from her leg.

"What?"

"What am I to you?" she asked, looking straight into his eyes.

"What are you talking about?" he said, pulling his hand away.

"Come on, don't make me spell it out for you."

"Spell what out?"

Amber sighed with frustration as she stood up.

"Okay, okay, okay. Wait! I'm sorry. I'm sorry I haven't called you."

"That's it?" Amber said, turning towards him. "That's all you've got?"

"What? I don't know what else you want from me."

"I want you to acknowledge that there is another person in the room with you."

"Are you serious?"

"Yes, I'm fucking serious!"

"Alright. I see you—I see you standing there." James extended his hands for emphasis.

"Do you? Do you really?"

"Okay, now I'm super confused."

"James, you slept with me—we slept together and now you completely ignore me. You've acted like I don't even exist, like I'm some girl you just picked up at a bar." Amber paused to gauge James' reaction. "How do you think that makes me feel?" Tears welled up in her eyes.

"I don't—I don't know."

"Exactly! And you didn't spend much time to figure it out, did you?"

James couldn't generate an answer.

"Let me ask you this: why did you call me tonight?"

"Uh, I was just responding to your text. You texted me."

"That's right; I did text you first. But why did you text me back? Why did you call and ask me to come over?"

"Alright, you're going a little crazy here. If I didn't call you, you'd be mad. And if I do call you, apparently you get mad? So, what am I supposed to do?"

"First of all, I'm not mad because you called. I'm mad because I know why you called."

"And why is that?"

"I'm getting there, but are you really that blind? Do

you really not recognize what you're doing, or are you just not honest with yourself? Or with me? Or with anyone?"

"I may not always be a great guy, but I'm no liar."

"I believe that, James. I really do. But not being a liar and being honest are two different things. Just like being honest and knowing the truth are two different things." Amber paused a moment. "I know us girls can be pretty complex, or 'crazy' as you might say, but guys are usually pretty simple. And I know what a guy who's been drinking wants at midnight, especially when he's gotten it before."

"So, why'd you come over?" James asked softly.

"Because I wanted to be wrong."

The strength of Amber's words seemed to shut the door on the conversation. James could only stare down at the couch with heavy eyes. He had never seen Amber this animated or angry or speaking with such conviction.

"I need a drink."

"Yeah," Amber sighed, backing towards James's recliner before plopping down.

James walked into the kitchen to fix two drinks, letting silence reign for several moments, apart from the clink of ice against glass.

James returned to the living room and offered Amber a glass. She accepted without looking up at him. Her eyes were dry now, but reddened.

James sat on the couch.

A few minutes later, James broke their uncomfortable silence. "What do we do now?" Amber simply shook her head, staring at the ice cubes that skated in a circular fashion within her drink.

Ah, I think I had too many.

*   *   *

Hours before his first high school dance, James watched, chin tucked, as his mother showed him how to properly tie a tie.

"See? Then you pull this end to slide the knot up, and you pull this end to tighten it," James' mother instructed.

"Ow, mom, that's too tight."

"Nonsense. You don't want to look like some slouch, do you? This is how it's supposed to look," she said as she turned his shoulders toward his reflection in the mirror. "Ah, look at that. My boy is so handsome."

"I'm not a boy, mom!"

"You're right, you're right. You're a young man now. And you're <u>my</u> young man, which is why I wish you would have asked Summer Walsh to the dance." Summer Walsh grew up winning beauty pageants as a child, was now a varsity cheerleader, and being a full year older than James in school made her seemingly out of his league. James's mother vaguely knew Summer's parents through mutual friends and always thought her to be the perfect match for her son.

"Why would you say something like that mom? I'm going with Kristen whether you like it or not, and if I don't leave soon, I'm gonna be late," James answered with teenaged impatience.

"I know. I know. I just think you could do better. I mean, Kristen is nice I guess, but Summer is gorgeous and popular—"

"Are you done?" James asked, turning to his mother. "Or do you want to ruin the whole night for me?"

"I just don't want you to make a habit out of settling. Look where it got me with your father."

James couldn't remember anything about his father. His mother had asked for a divorce when James was two.

"I know, mom. I hear you. Can I go now?" James asked, taking one more glance in the mirror, this time more confident.

At the end of that night, James gave Kristen a good night kiss in front of her house, but they never went on another date.

Friday

James's alarm sounded at 7:00am. Upon first movement, his head felt like a fire station at the bottom of the ocean: all ringing and immense pressure. He squirmed in his bed, groaning miserably, realizing full well that he had to work two jobs that day. *Ahhh, fuck me.* Fortunately, or unfortunately, depending on how you look at it, James had experienced similar pain plenty of times before and knew that to remedy the situation he would need a hot shower, a starchy breakfast, and some Gatorade. James did his best to administer all three treatments and arrived at *Idyll* a few minutes before 9:00am.

Fridays at the paper were slow. Days like this made the industry of printed news feel even nearer to extinction. James only waited for tumbleweeds to blow through the office and make it more of a ghost town. James might have seen potential for his next article amid these ideas if he wasn't so anxiously awaiting Tori's arrival. He had never been so mystified by a woman's behavior. At one moment she seemed to crave him, and then the next moment she disappeared with no warning and absolutely no communication. *It's not like I like this girl, but what the hell is wrong with her?* As James brooded in front of his computer screen, Lauren Duvall approached his cubicle.

"Hey, James, got a minute?"

"Yeah, of course," James answered, minimizing the pages on his desktop.

"Would you like to step into my office? I'd rather speak with you there."

"Sure."

Lauren could make a fundamentalist, Islamic terrorist turn pacifist and an avid capitalist Christian with just a few sentences from his rich, soothing baritone. He was instantly trustworthy, and everyone liked him.

"I want to let you know about a job opportunity," Lauren said after they had seated themselves on either side of his desk.

"Okay."

"My good friend is editor in chief of *Northwest Metropolitan*. It's an offshoot of the *Seattle Met* that's being well received in its infant stage. Have you heard of it?"

"Yeah, I've skimmed through it a few times. It's nice."

"Well, they're in need of a beat reporter. Apparently, they want to expand their lifestyles section to include the nightlife of cities in the northwest. They say they want someone who is in tune with that scene and sensitive to the nature of their demographic, which is essentially the offspring of baby boomers. I naturally thought of you. You're the perfect age and you work at the restaurant. I thought it would be a perfect fit. What do you think?"

"Wow! I'm really honored that you thought of me, first of all. I really appreciate that. Umm, it definitely sounds intriguing—"

"There's no need to answer right now," Lauren interjected.

"Oh, okay."

"I just wanted to let you know. Take the week to think about it; get back to me when you've had a chance to digest it."

"Okay, I will," James paused a moment. "It's based out of—"

"Seattle. Yes, you would be required to move."

"Oh, well, Seattle is a cool town."

"Yeah, I love the whole Puget Sound area. My sister lives up there. It's beautiful."

"Okay, well, I guess I have a lot to think about over the weekend," James said with smile.

"It's a big opportunity. I'd hate to lose you, but I think you deserve it."

"I appreciate that. Thank you."

"Well, we'd better get back to work," Lauren stood to shake hands.

"Yeah, I guess you're right."

"Alright, take care, James."

"Thanks, you too."

James drifted back to his desk, mulling over the idea of picking up and moving to Seattle while reflecting on the fact that he had spent his whole life in Arbor Valley. *Seattle is a cool town. Besides, what the fuck am I leaving behind here?*

Where the fuck is Tori?

James spent most of the morning scanning several blogs looking for ways that the economy had affected the local art scene, a special request of Janet. But every time someone came through the doors, James's eyes jumped up to see if it was Tori. James felt awkwardly troubled by her absence, but he did his best to hide this from his coworkers, especially Brian. He even thought up elaborate explanations, however unnecessary, in case his demeanor was called into question. After hours of unfocused work, he finally went to talk with Janet.

"Are you busy?" James asked as he lightly knocked on her open door.

"No, come on in."

"I'm having a little trouble finding good information on this local art situation."

"Oh yeah? What seems to be the problem?"

"Well, people seem to be mentioning their frustrations in very subtle, sort of—tangential ways. I feel like, if I quote somebody, I'd be taking things way out of context. You know, taking too much liberty."

"I think I know what you're saying."

"Yeah, I just want to make this sound right. If this kind of piece is what I'm going to do, I want to make sure I don't misrepresent any of these artists."

"So, how do you think I can help?"

"Well, I thought you might know someone. I mean, you seem to be tapped into that sort of thing. I thought you might know someone I could talk to—personally."

"You mean an interview?"

"Yeah, I guess."

"Hmmm. Let me think on that one and I'll get back to you—in a little bit," Janet said, gesturing with her hands that he could leave.

"Oh, okay. Thanks," James answered before turning

midstride. "Do you know where Tori is today?"

"She called in sick. Why?"

"Oh, no reason. I was just curious. Well, I'll talk to you in a bit."

"Okay, I'll let you know."

James eluded productivity after lunch as well. Federal initiatives created to give small business owners tax breaks for manufacturing goods in the U.S. and how that related to the local art industry's recent struggles could only hold James's attention for so long. His mind was in a state of agitation: convoluted by punk music and Space Needles and crying girls and dehydration and the color red and coffee shops and drunken texts...

James left the office by 2:00pm after getting the name of a Cynthia Larkin from Janet. He bought a 22oz bottle of Long Hammer IPA on the way home, put *London Calling* in his CD player, and tried working in his journal from the recliner that still smelled like Amber's perfume before heading to Un Monde Parfait. He fell asleep before any ideas came to him worth writing.

James awoke to a bottle he chose to view as half full, looked at his phone, and decided it was time to get ready to leave. James lathered up for a quick shave, a premeditated ritual on nights he worked with Ally, and was out the door with an empty stomach.

Friday nights at Un Monde Parfait started slowly. The early arriving couples in their mid-fifties carefully peruse the menu behind thin glasses, only to order unlisted items. Their salt and peppered hair, Joseph A. Bank polos, and sweaters from Talbots distinguish them from their servers and the later arriving crowds. By 8:00pm a flood of thirty-somethings fill all empty seats. Soon their conversations compete for air space and intellectual supremacy between sips of Waterbrook cabernet, and cask conditioned ale, and Bombay Sapphire gin & tonics, and Tullamore Dew whiskey. They all listen to Dave Matthews Band and ask for couscous with their almond encrusted trout.

James walked in at 5:57pm with the restaurant at about half capacity. He went straight to the back to clock in.

"Hey, how's it goin'?" Tony asked, passing by on his way to the bar.

"Good. Hey, who's workin' tonight?"

"Ah—it's you, Ally, Luis, and Megan out on the floor, and Claire and I at the bar."

"Is Dan here?"

"Yeah, for another couple of hours. Why?"

"I just need to ask him something. I might need to go to an interview in Seattle."

"Really? Nice! Well, I got to get back out there. We'll talk in a bit, okay?"

"Yeah, alright." James punched his employee number into the POS and began putting on his apron when Luis came back to enter an order. "Hey, how are you?"

"Oh, I'm fine," he said with a sigh. "I think that lady over there is racist though."

"Which one? The one in the white blouse?"

"Yeah."

"What makes you say that?"

"Just the way she looks at me."

"That's it? Don't you think you're being a little paranoid?"

"No, I can tell she thinks I'm some wetback."

"You always think people are racist."

"Because they are."

"Do you want me to spill something on her?"

"You're very funny."

"I try to be."

"I'll be fine, thanks," Luis said, turning to leave.

James scanned the dining area waiting for new customers to arrive. *Ally must not be on until 7:00.*

The night started rather uneventfully. Ally showed up and James tried to avoid sounding too flirtatious when he complemented her on her hair. He told their manager Dan that he might have to get the following Friday off in order to fly to Seattle. And, like usual, he wanted to kill a few of the customers. Dan left before 8:00pm and soon after Tony motioned for James to join him out back.

"When's the last time you did blow?" Tony asked as he opened the door for James.

"I've never done 'blow'."

"What?"

"Yeah, why would I?"

"Because your girlfriend left you for another woman," Tony replied. This would have seemed like a random comment if Tony's girlfriend of three years hadn't broken up with him six months ago and declared that she was gay.

"Good point," James answered, "but didn't you do it before then?"

"Touché."

"Hey, welcome to the party!" Eric said as James and Tony stepped outside. "Come pull up a chair, or a box, or something-or-other." Eric was joined by Steve, a cook who worked on the weekends, and the other waitress, Megan. The two newcomers helped shape a small, half circle.

"Is anyone still working?" James asked.

"Why, is it busy?" Eric answered.

"They'll be alright," Tony said with assurance.

"That's what you always say, Costa, that's why you're such a chill manager," Megan said.

Well, Megan's already high.

"It's because I've reached enlightenment, Megan. Some day you'll learn." Megan laughed at Tony's straight-faced delivery. "Now who wants some of this?" Tony said as he pulled out a plastic bag from his pocket.

"Me."

"I'm in."

"Me too."

"What about you, James?" Tony asked.

"No thanks."

"Are you sure, Jamie-Stay-Clean?"

"Yeah, I'm sure."

"Well, at least have some of this," Steve said, tossing James a bottle of Wild Turkey.

"Now <u>that</u> I can do." James unscrewed the cap to the bottle of bourbon as Tony measured lines on a silver baking tray from the kitchen. James took a pull from the bottle and winced. The liquid was warm and stale, and the after taste burned like lighter fluid. "Man, how did Hunter S. Thompson drink so much of this shit?"

"Who?" Megan asked.

"Never mind," James replied.

"He used to work here," Tony added.

"Oh, cool," Megan said. The guys all exchanged crooked smiles.

"Alright, here we go. Go ahead and start us off Megan," Tony said, passing the tray and a pre-cut straw.

"Aren't you guys a little sketchy about someone just walking up? I mean it's pretty hard to pass that off as something else," James said.

"Nah, no one walks back here at this time of night. The drunks aren't out yet," Eric replied.

"Plus, we could just say we were doing a taste test," Steve said with a childish grin as he accepted the tray from Megan.

I thought Megan would be the only one saying dumb shit.

Tony lit a cigarette as he waited his turn. James took another pull from the bottle.

"So, what's this about you going to Seattle?" Tony asked.

"It's a job interview for a magazine."

"Oh, yeah? That sounds pretty legit. How did this all happen?"

"My boss just gave this guy my name."

"Wow, Seattle! You should go!" Megan chimed in.

"Well, I plan on going to the job interview."

"No, I mean you should take the job. Seattle is so cool."

"Well, I haven't exactly been offered the job."

"Still though—" And, at that moment, Ally came through the door. Eric hid the baking tray behind his back.

"Can someone come help us in here?" Ally said with slight agitation in her voice.

"I'm coming," Megan said as she quickly jumped up.

"I'll be there in a second too," James said. *Don't make her angry.*

After the door closed, Tony asked Eric if he was finished with his turn.

"Yeah, here you go."

"So, James, if they offer you the job, are you taking it?" Tony asked just before he snorted up his line.

"I don't know. I haven't had that much time to think about it really."

"Can you think—of a good—reason not to?" Tony asked while trying to clear his nose.

Don't say Ally. Don't say Ally. "No, not really."

"I can hook you up with some people from the band I used to play with," Eric said.

"Thanks, man," James replied.

"Hey, sorry to change the subject, but when is someone going to fuck Megan?" Steve interjected.

"Alright, that's my cue to leave. You guys have fun. I'm going back to work," James said as he stood up to leave. He listened to the last few bits of their conversation until the door swung shut behind him.

"Are you kidding? She's not attractive."

"Plus, she's like half your age."

"So, what..."

As it crept past 11:00pm, the restaurant began to clear out. James noticed Ally clearing one of the now several empty tables and took the opportunity to talk to her.

"Here, let me help," he said, picking up the table's

center piece.

"Oh, thanks."

"Busy night, huh?"

"Oh my god," she replied with a frustrated fatigue and proceeded to wipe down the table.

"That bad?"

"No, I'm just tired, you know?"

"Yeah, I know what you mean. This is the second job I've worked today, and I started the day hung-over."

"Wow. I guess I shouldn't complain," she said, attempting to adjust her hair with the back of her hand and wrist. "You worked at the paper today too?"

"You can complain if you want. I can't say that I worked very hard—at either job." James set down the center piece.

"Are you always so self-deprecating?"

"I don't know. Maybe just around you."

"Oh, yeah?" she said with a coquettish tilt of the head. "Can you help me with this one too?"

"As you wish."

While walking to the next table, Ally threw him a curious glance, as if she just then got the reference. *I love the way she walks.*

"Any big weekend plans, or do you have to work the whole time?" Ally asked.

"No, I'm off tomorrow. As far as plans go, I don't think I have any. How 'bout you?"

"Actually, tomorrow night is one of my best friends' bachelorette parties!"

"Ooh, that sounds fun."

"Yeah, we're going dancing," Ally gestured little dance moves with her upper body as she spoke, "I'll probably shake my thing a little bit," she said with a bounce of her hips, "and I'll probably have one too many cosmopolitans."

"I'd like to see that."

"I bet you would." Ally giggled and lightly touched James's arm. James smiled in response.

"So, where is all this taking place?"

"I think we're starting at The Peach, and then we'll probably end up bouncing around a little bit. Our friend Sandra has it all planned out, supposedly."

"The Peach, eh? That's the place that plays The Beatles set to techno."

"You've been there?"

"I've walked by."

"Beatles songs set to techno, huh? That sounds cool."

Please tell me you didn't just say that. "If sacrilege is cool."

"Oh, stop. You're one of those snobby purists aren't you?"

"I try to be," James said with a smirk.

"Well, thanks for the help. I better get back to my tables."

"Yeah, me too. And you're welcome." James paused to watch her walk away. *Maybe instead of her birthday it should be her measurements? Nah...*

Saturday

James pulled up to Cynthia Larkin's house just before 10:00am on Saturday morning. It was a simple off-white house in one the original neighborhoods in Arbor Valley; a set of stone steps led up to the front door and a raised foundation: a quintessential 1940's architectural design. The property was nestled in thick shade from massive oaks and cottonwoods, while over-grown shrubs surrounding the house gave it a slightly unkempt appearance.

James ascended the steps and rang the doorbell. *I hope she remembers I was coming today.* After a few long seconds, James finally heard muffled feet on hard wood.

"Ah, good morning," she said opening the front door, eyes adjusting to the sun light beneath square, graying bangs.

"Good morning, Ms. Larkin, I'm James Dall. It's nice to meet you," he said, extending his hand.

"It's nice to meet you too, James. Please, call me Cynthia. Formality makes me feel even older than I am. Come on in."

"Thank you."

"You can have a seat wherever you like. Do you drink

coffee?"

"Yeah, I drink—"

"Good, I'll get you a cup."

"Okay, thanks," James said as he took a seat on an old catcher's mitt of a couch.

Cynthia walked down the hall to her kitchen. "Have you ever had homegrown coffee before?"

"I can't say that I have."

"My neighbor grows it in his basement. It's delicious stuff."

What else does he grow in his basement? "Well, I'm eager to try it."

"Do you take cream or sugar?"

"Both please." *Just like Mr. Wolf.*

After the sounds of pouring and stirring and refrigerator doors opening and closing, Cynthia reappeared with two giant mugs of coffee. "Here you go."

"Thank you very much."

"Now, tell me again what kind of information you thought I could help you with. I know you told me something on the phone yesterday, but I don't quite remember," Cynthia said as she sat down opposite of James, carefully crossing her legs inside a long, burgundy prairie skirt.

"Well, basically, my story is about the recession's effect on local artists."

"Ah, yes. Janet said something about that too."

Great. What else did Janet say? "So, yeah. I thought you could give me some specifics, to lend it authenticity and, honestly, make life easier on me."

"Well, I'll sure do anything I can. I'm happy to help."

"I appreciate that. Now, do you mind if I record our

conversation?" James asked, pulling out his tape recorder.

"No, I don't mind. I just won't mention anything about San Francisco in the 70's or my plan to take down Reagan in the 80's." James was visibly caught off guard. "I'm kidding," Cynthia assured.

"Oh, okay," James replied with a smile.

"Well, at least a little bit."

"I guess I'll start by asking, 'how dependent are you on the selling of your art for income?' "

"Ooh, that's a good one. I'd have to say 'almost completely.' "

"How much do—"

"But that depends on what you mean by 'dependent'." As she spoke, her eyes drifted up towards the heavily textured ceiling, as if she was reading invisible cue cards. "See, I depend on my art as a way of living, so to speak, but the way I choose to see it is my art depends on me. If I didn't create it, if I didn't bring it to life, who else would? So, you see? It needs me more than I need it. But I suppose it is a mutual thing."

"That's an interesting way to look at it, I guess."

"Well, that's the secret, James."

"What?"

"Looking at things," Cynthia said with her eyes momentarily fixed on James. "Looking at things differently. Looking at things under a different light. Looking at things from the light." Her eyes bounced around the room at various objects.

"But what's it the secret to?"

Cynthia paused to take a sip of coffee before answering. "Everything."

"Everything," James repeated as he scrawled a few

things on his notepad. As he underlined a few key words, a fluffy, gray cat jumped onto the couch and curled itself under James' right elbow.

"Oh, I'm sorry. You can push him down if you want. Ernst, get down!"

"It's okay. How 'bout you just scoot over there, little buddy," James said, carefully escorting the cat with the back of his hand. Ernst took the gesture for affection, leaned in, and purred.

"Are you allergic? Sorry, I should have asked when you came in."

"Not that I'm aware of."

"Good. I just can't believe there are people out there who are allergic to companionship. Ernst here is my social one. And O'Keeffe is probably hiding around here somewhere. She's relatively shy."

"Not to change the subject, but going back to my first question..."

"Oh yes, I'm sorry."

"If you don't mind, about how much do you make from selling your art per month?"

"On average?"

"Yes."

"Well, of course every month is different. Some months, I don't sell anything, but if I'm lucky enough to be in a good show I can make a few thousand dollars in a night. On average though," she counted on her fingers, "I'd have to say about fifteen hundred."

"Has that number fluctuated much in, let's say, the last five years?"

"No, not really. I guess you'd expect things to slow down a little if everyone is having to tighten their belts and 'reduce superfluous spending,' as they say, but it hasn't."

"Why do you think that is?"

"I just don't think people get tired of being inspired. We can put a price tag on a piece of art after we analyze its size, and the types of materials used, and if we've ever sold anything like it before, but you can't really put a price tag on what it means to someone."

James added to his notes. "What about these pieces? Are they all yours?" James pointed to the paintings and sculptures that lined the sage green walls of the living room.

"Oh, no. I don't hang up much of my own artwork. At least not out here. Most of that is friends' work."

"So, how much did you pay for some of these?"

"Oh, we don't buy each other's things, for the most part. We do a lot of trading."

"I see."

"If you'd like to see my things, I could show you out back."

"Sure, I'd like that, if you don't mind."

"Not at all."

Cynthia led James down the hall, past bedroom doors, and in between the kitchen and dining area. "That last room on the right there is where I work if I'm inside, but I try to spend most of my time out here." She opened the back door and they stepped out into an enclosed patio: a sort of rustic sunroom littered with easels, stretcher bars, cans of brushes, stacks of finished and unfinished work, bottles of paint, palettes, a pottery wheel, and even a kiln. "Here's my beautiful mess."

"Wow! This is impressive."

"Well, I don't know about that, but thank you."

"This kind of leads me to my next question," James said glancing back at his notes. "If your income has remained relatively steady over the last few years, have you noticed any difference in the cost of supplies?"

"Not really. I mean, a lot of the petroleum-based products are more expensive than they used to be, but, for the most part, that stuff doesn't really affect me. You just learn to be more resourceful. Frugality is one of the hidden blessings to living the artist's life."

"I bet." James fingered his way through a stack of paintings like they were vinyl records. "How do you find time to work out here as much as you do?"

"I don't 'find' time as much as I 'make' time."

"Can you explain that a little?"

"James, do you have a woman?"

"What? No."

"A man?"

"Oh, no, I like women. I just don't have one."

"You don't have one or you don't know which one to choose?"

"I'm not sure I follow."

"Picture your dream girl. Now, are you going to try to find some time to be with her, or are you going to make time for her?"

"I see."

"It's about priorities. If you're going to be an artist, you have to be married to your art. I'm like a nun, except canvas and oil paint is my god," Cynthia said, making herself laugh.

James wrote down the words 'married to your art' and underlined them.

The rest of the interview dissolved into a casual conversation about art, Cynthia's mostly, with which James seemed satisfied, bringing an end to all economics related questions. When Cynthia noticed the time, she began to usher James towards the front door.

"I'm sorry to rush you out the door. The time just snuck up on me, and I have to get ready for my art students," Cynthia said with a hurried flutter to her voice.

"You teach out of your home?"

"Yeah, a few days a week," she said as the heavy door groaned upon opening. "Just enough to stay busy."

"Well, I'll get out of your hair then," he said, pushing open the screen. "Thanks again for the interview. It was really nice meeting you."

"It was nice to meet you too. I just hope I was able to help you."

"Oh, I think the story will turn out fine," James said, descending the steps.

"I'm sure it will."

James grabbed a window seat at Colter's Saloon at 8:10pm. The name gave the impression of a grizzly, small town bar in some remote mountain location, scaring away most casual drinkers, but Colter's actually laid on Arbor Valley's main strip of downtown bars and their true niche, or specialty, was their premium selection of scotch, bourbon, and Canadian whiskeys. Colter's loyal customer base consisted of men in their forties or fifties who either had a lot of money to spend or, like James, simply chose to spend a lot of money to get drunk.

I can't believe I've stayed sober until now.

"Are you waiting for someone else?" the waiter asked.

"No."

"Here's a drink menu. I'll be back with some water."

"Thanks."

James found the pastoral ambiance to be a peaceful place to begin any night of drinking. The rich smell of oak and finished pine, the smoky warm embrace of scotch going down, and the framed Ansel Adams pictures of Yellowstone hanging on the walls kindled a romantic solitude that James sought after. He thought of this serenity as part of his purchase, even though it never appeared on the itemized receipt.

"Here's your water. Do you know what you'd like?"

"Yeah, I'll have a glass of The Dalmore."

"We actually have the fifteen-year-old from them right now as well."

"No, thanks. I'll stick with the twelve."

"Okay, I'll be right back with that."

Sitting near windows with a good view was a ritual for James dating back to college. Finding a private alcove on the third floor of the university library where he could overlook students passing through the quad was an essential way to study and kill time between classes. James loved analyzing people; he believed they always revealed their true selves when they didn't know anyone was watching. Insecure individuals uncomfortably wait for someone to join them, quarreling couples wear their disgust for each other in the shapes of crossed arms, furrowed brows, and exasperated looks to the heavens; and all guys mentally grope every attractive woman walking by.

"Here's your Dalmore. Can I get you anything else?"

"Nope. I think I'm good. Thanks." James picked up the

glass and held it to his nose. *Hello beautiful.* After a slow whiff of the spicy orange aroma, James took his first sip of vanilla and sherry wood. *Whew! I feel better already.*

On this particular night, the reason Colter's Saloon was such an ideal place for people watching was because it stood directly across from The Peach.

James surveyed the sidewalks on either side of Main Street, one lying along the side of Colter's and the other stretching across the front of The Peach and its neighboring bars. The saloon's large windows provided a thin layer of protection from the outside world, a sense of invincibility analogous to the glossy film of an intoxicated eye. And in that way, James soon felt twice as comfortable.

He passed the time through a combination of scrutinizing the passersby, sending a few texts in case his plan fell through, and reading the contents of the drink menu, all while never taking his eyes off the entrance to The Peach for more than five to ten seconds at a time.

The drink menu was an elaborate publication full of detailed information on everything from whiskey ingredients to the distilling process. Each page even included a witty quote about drinking from a famous person. Yes, the ones that help rationalize the very reason you're sitting there. James especially enjoyed these.

A sleeveless lime green silk blouse and black mini skirt. *Please don't walk away. Come back.*

James texted Tony Costa, "What are you up to tonight?".

Frank Sinatra said, "I feel sorry for people who don't drink. When they wake up in the morning, that's as good as they're going to feel all day".

Two graphic print dress shirts, three button holes open, with gelled spiky hair. *I wonder if they get tired of being douche-bags.*

No answer from Tony yet.

"A whiskey is only as good as its base ingredients (barley, water, yeast, etc.)," the menu said.

James sucked the last watered-down bit of whiskey from his glass. "Can I get you another one of those?" the waiter asked as he walked towards the table.

"Yes, please," James answered. The waiter stopped midstride, turned heel-toe, and went to the bar.

Layers of what looked like soft serve poured into tight jeans and a white t-shirt two sizes too small. A muffin top pulled the outfit together. *Oh God! Why?*

"Tony texted back, "Drinking at home. going out later, u?".

James replied, "I'm hanging out with friends. I'll hit you up if we go to a place you'd enjoy."

Hemingway said, "An intelligent man is sometimes forced to be drunk to spend time with his fools."

"Here you go, sir," the waiter said politely.

"Oh, thank you." James took a sip from his new drink. *What's keeping this damn bachelorette party?*

A group of retro tank tops, cut off jean shorts, and Vans. *Now you have to spend money to look like trash.*

James texted Cade, "Are you free tonight? Want to get a drink?".

"A good whiskey is the product of several successful chemical reactions," the menu said.

A printed baby-doll top and white pants perfectly draped the curves of a brown skinned beauty. *I bet she tastes like heaven.*

James took a long drink.

Cade texted back, "If you asked earlier, I would have. We're watching a movie. Sorry."

James Joyce said, "The light music of whiskey falling into a glass—an agreeable interlude."

And in this manner, James killed the next hour or so.

"How are you doin'? Ready for another?" the waiter asked.

"No, thanks. I think I'm ready for the bill," James said as he retrieved his debit card.

"Okay, I'll be right back."

This has been a fuckin' waste of time. At least the whiskey's good. James chewed the ice from his fourth drink. Suddenly, with a fatigued attentiveness, he noticed a group of women walk out of The Peach and huddle up in front of the entrance. There were six or seven of them encircling a little brunette in a white top and a silver, plastic tiara. James racked his focus and peered into the group. The sun was beginning to go down and details were harder to make out. Just then, a blonde in a turquoise halter top cocktail dress stepped out of the bar and joined them. It was Ally. James' jaw dropped, an ice cube hit the floor, and James turned in his seat to locate the waiter. *Where is he? I've got to go!*

James scrambled to his feet in a subdued panic. He took short, quick breaths through his mouth, panning his head back and forth between the window and the waiter's last known location.

Finally, the waiter came back with the bill. "Here you

go, sir. Thanks for comin' in."

"Thank you," James said bending over the table, too drunk to do the math in his head. *Seven plus six equals three, carry the one.* He looked at the total. *Shit, there goes a night's worth of tips.* As he slid his debit card back into his wallet, he noticed Ally's party start moving from his right to the left. James pressed his face up to the glass to better his viewing angle, unaware of how peculiar he looked. *They're crossing the street!* And with that, James bolted out of Colter's and onto 6th Street.

As James turned right, he noticed Ally and her friends continuing to walk down Main Street. He crossed 6th and followed them from the other side of Main, staying about fifty yards behind. The smell of bratwursts and grilled onions teased him as he kept a watchful eye. After about a block, the women turned to go into Club Velvet, a small city's attempt to be a big city dance club. James turned around and bought a bottled water from the hot dog vendor. *I'll give 'em a few minutes before I go in.*

James bided his time by walking around the block and trying to rehydrate, thinking of a way to script his 'chance encounter' with Ally.

When James walked up to the front entrance at 10:05pm, a small line had formed. The bouncers checked IDs and looked people up and down. James couldn't remember if they had a dress code, but he figured they needed his business. *Hey, at least I put on a polo today.*

"ID?" a bouncer asked.

"Yep."

Thumping bass snuck out of the door each time someone was admitted.

"Alright, he'll stamp your hand."

James shuffled forward.

"It'll be ten dollars," another bouncer barked.

"What?"

"Yeah, it's a ten dollar cover Saturdays after 10:00."

"Alright. Well, there's all the cash I have."

"There's an ATM inside," the bouncer said as he unhooked a velvet movie theater rope.

"That really makes you feel special, huh?"

The bouncer had no rebuttal, he simply watched James open the door and walk inside.

As soon as James crossed the threshold, he entered another world: a world of constant vibrations, a sort of techno defibrillator. Blue and purple overhead lights showered all vision, erasing all bad complexion. The strobe carved everybody's movements into a flipbook soaked with mixed drinks.

There were several bars to choose from, but James headed to the nearest one. He grabbed the attention of a bartender with blue eye shadow.

"What would you like?" she said over the music.

James leaned in. "What beers do you have on tap?"

"We have Bud, Bud Light, Budweiser Select, Miller Lite, Heineken, Blue Moon—"

"What's that one right there from Deschutes?" James interrupted.

"Oh, let me see." She stepped back to peer at the tap handle. "Mirror Pond."

"I'll have that." *It's the only thing worth drinking here.*

After receiving his beer, James went upstairs and stood on the catwalk that overlooked the dance floor. *It can't be that hard to find her.* James sipped his drink slowly.

W.C. Fields said, "A woman drove me to drink and I never even had the courtesy to thank her."

A couple of songs and a half beer later, James spotted Ally's group dancing together. Only now did he notice they were all wearing similar shades of teal or aqua blue, except, of course, for the bride to be. James fixated on Ally, and rightfully so. Her long blonde hair guided sight to the sharp V-neck of her dress, plunging deep to a high beaded waist. As she moved, the chiffon skirt flowed about her in elegant waves. *God, she's amazing!*

James caught himself in a gaze and decided to move down to the dance floor. He slammed the last of his beer and left the empty glass on someone's table at the bottom of the stairs. James's strategy was to slink his way along the wall, towards the front of the dance floor, and then drift his way back through the mass of dancing bodies, eventually into Ally's, making it seem like an accident they met there.

James entered the dance floor feeling comfortable. The whiskey in his veins moved him with a certain fluidity. When a new song started, James scooted in the bachelorette party's direction, taking quick peeks to be sure. Before long, his plan seemed to work.

"James." He forced himself to ignore it the first time. "James. Hey, James," Ally shouted.

"Hey, what's up?" James forced a look of surprise as he turned and moved closer.

"Nothin'. We're out for my friend's bachelorette party."

"What?" James asked, cupping his ear.

She leaned in close. "My friend is getting married. This is her bachelorette party."

"Oh, Awesome!" The smell of Ally's perfume made James's voice quiver.

"What are <u>you</u> doing here?"

"I came here with some friends, but I think they might have bailed on me."

"Hey, this is Katelyn," Ally said, gesturing to another girl in teal dancing beside them.

"Hi, nice to meet you. I'm James." James shook her hand.

"Nice to meet you too."

"So, what's the deal with all the matching colors?" James asked, directing his focus back to Ally.

"We're supposed to be the ocean."

"What?"

"It's the theme of the party." James shook his head in confusion. "She's originally from the coast and her fiancé is in the Navy. It just all ties together."

"Why is she wearing white?"

"Because she has to stand out."

"It's not because she's the precious pearl this guy found in the midst of the deep blue sea?" James asked jokingly.

"No, but that it is a good idea." Ally smiled. "I'll tell her."

"Well, ocean or not, you look beautiful in that dress." *Just keep her smiling.*

"Ah, thank you. You sure I don't look like I'm at the prom?"

"I don't know how to answer that."

"Oh, I was just a little worried that—"

"Let me put it this way: your prom date is a lucky guy."

"You're too sweet."

James replied with a simple shrug.

"Hey, you should come have a drink with us after this song. We've got a VIP room all to ourselves."

"Are you sure guys are welcome?"

"Yeah. I mean, just for a little while." Ally smiled and touched his arm.

The VIP room was about the size of James' whole apartment if you knocked out all the walls. It had its own private bar and a pool table in the middle. The perimeter was lined with comfy chairs, couches, and green plastic plants. Low-level lighting of warm gold replaced the strobe and fluorescent rainbow of the dance floor.

"At least now we don't have to scream over the music," Ally said.

"Yeah, I'm about to lose my voice," James replied.

"Let me introduce you to everybody."

"Okay."

"This is Sandra, Lisa, you met Katelyn, Rachelle," James waved as Ally pointed around the room. "That's Amina, and here is the soon-to-be-married-woman, Krystal. Everybody, this is James. We work together at Un Monde Parfait."

"Hi, James," echoed a multitude of shrill voices.

"Nice to meet you all," James said.

"He should get the next kiss," Rachelle blurted out.

"Yeah, what's the tally at?"

"That's a great idea," Ally said.

"She's on her fifth drink and she's only had three kisses," Sandra said, reading from her phone.

"Huh?" James mumbled, head swiveling to locate the

source of each comment.

"Krystal has to kiss a guy for every drink she has. It's one of her challenges," Ally explained.

"And we're going to keep her drinking all night long!"

"Because she's been such a prude all her life!"

"You ready?" Ally asked.

"Sure." James swallowed. "I mean, of course." *At least she's fairly cute.*

"Go lay one on him," Sandra said to Krystal.

"Just a peck though, James. No funky stuff," Ally giggled.

This is seventh grade spin the bottle all over again.

James leaned in to kiss the shorter Krystal with pursed, platonic lips. The women all cheered in unison.

"Nicely done! That makes four," Sandra said. "Someone get her another drink!"

"That's a lot of pressure with everybody watching," James said to Ally with a smirk.

"Oh yeah? Well, thanks for being a good sport then. I'm sure you don't mind kissing cute girls <u>too</u> much," Ally replied.

"No. No, I don't." *But you don't know the half of it.*

"You want another drink?"

"You read my mind."

Ally ordered a gin and tonic and James had another Mirror Pond in an attempt to slow himself down. The women talked about people and events with which James was unfamiliar, so he resorted to sipping his beer and smiling politely. He noticed Tony had texted him back, but James didn't bother reading or responding to the message.

"Hey, you want to go back down and dance?" Ally asked James as she finished her drink.

"Sure. Just let me finish this beer," James said.

"Yeah, hurry up slow poke. I thought you were a real drinker like everyone else from work."

"I had some before I came."

"Excuses, excuses," Ally said, placing her hands on her hips as part of a coquettish reprimand.

"Yes ma'am," James answered and tilted back his beer.

"Don't say that. It makes me feel old."

"Alright, young lady, let's go tear up the dance floor." As James stood up, he felt his sixth drink. His head felt like an old medicine ball filled with sand. Balance was hampered. Walking in slender S's was now the only option.

"Do you guys want to come down?" Ally asked of her friends.

"Not right now. We'll be down there in a bit."

"Shall we?" James said, extending a gentlemanly bent arm.

"Yes, sir." Ally responded, linking her arm in his.

Talk about a dream come true...

The dance floor was even more crowded than before. James paused before entering the sweaty mass of humanity, but Ally said, "Come on!" and beckoned him with her hand. They passed through clouds of Axe body spray and sticky patches of dried Vodka Red Bulls until they found enough space for them to dance.

"I think they're still playing the same song," James stressed his voice as they began moving to the beat.

"No, this is a different one. I think it's—"

"I was joking."

"Oh, okay," Ally laughed. James could tell she didn't get it.

"I think you're taller than me in those heels."

"You think so?"

"Yeah, I'm surprised you can move so well in 'em."

"Well, I've had lots of practice."

While they danced, James tried to inch his hips closer to Ally's as each song progressed but waited to see if she would reciprocate before moving in all the way.

"We should go see what's taking them so long," Ally said of her friends after a few songs.

"I'm sure they'll be down soon. Let me buy you a drink," James replied.

"Okay."

"After you," James gestured with his hand.

Ally led them to the bar nearest the dance floor. James noticed that, in Ally's company, they were served quickly.

"What would you like?" asked a square-jawed bartender.

"I'll have a gin and tonic," Ally said.

"Is Seagram's okay?"

"Yes."

"And for you?"

"I'll have a shot of Wild Turkey," James said.

William Blake once said, "The road of excess leads to the palace of wisdom."

"Are you guys together?" the bartender asked.

"Yeah, just put it all on my tab, please," James answered, choosing to hear a double meaning in the bartender's last question.

"Thanks for the drink," Ally said.

"It's my pleasure."

The bartender slid them their glasses, upon which Ally lifted hers saying, "Cheers!"

"To Un Monde Parfait," James responded, wishing the translation to be communicated in this instance, but knowing, of course, that Ally merely thought of the restaurant. James took his shot and Ally took long sips from her straw. James looked out onto the dance floor feeling like someone had torn out every other page from his flipbook-vision. People moved frenetically under the strobe. Just then, the song changed.

"Oh my God; I love this song!" Ally erupted. "Come on. Let's go." Ally set down her half-finished drink and pranced to the dance floor. James hurried after her. At the far end of the floor the lights cross faded between purples and blues, at eye level, cutting all bodies into two-dimensional silhouettes swimming in a neon tide.

Once in the middle of the dance floor, James centered his eyes on Ally's back. She danced facing the lights, as if to bathe in their vibrancy. James' closeness allowed him to see all of her dimensions: the delicate narrowing at her wrists, the perfect angle her elbows made as she ran her fingers through and lifted up her long hair, the gentle protrusion of her shoulder blades and the beads of sweat collecting between them, glistening from the strobe overhead.

Ally turned around wearing a blissful expression: eyes closed, grin euphoric. In one motion, James placed his hand at the small of her back and kissed her.

"No, James," Ally said pulling back, hands defensively on his chest.

"What?" James asked as Ally walked briskly off the

dance floor. He followed her through the crowd, grabbing her arm as she started up the stairs. "Wait! Can we talk for a second?"

"I can't believe you just did that!"

"Let me explain."

"What's there to explain? You can't go off kissing people who're practically engaged."

"But it's okay for me to kiss your friend, Krystal?"

"That's different."

"Oh yeah? How?"

"It just is."

"Well, has he proposed to you yet?"

"No, but that's not the point, James."

"What is the point?"

Ally took a calming breath. "James, I don't like you like that. Okay? And even if I wasn't with someone, I'd feel the same way." With that, Ally turned and ascended the staircase. James stood frozen, watching her with hollowness in his gut. *She didn't mean it.*

TRUTHS

Sunday

James reentered the sanctuary of Horizon View Baptist church near the beginning of a sermon on idolatry in the twenty-first century. Identifying the most suitable time to refill one's coffee at church had always been an ordeal for James. It's awkward to leave in the middle of worship, it's too quiet during announcements, and it feels extremely inappropriate during testimonies and baby dedications. James usually tried to capitalize on an elongated transition of some kind. Each church was different, though.

Once he returned to his seat, James tasted the coffee; it was strong, mirroring the aching in his head. He drifted off in thought, picturing Ally in her turquoise dress, as the pastor stressed the importance of learning from Israel's past mistakes.

"...If you turn your Bibles to 1 Corinthians 10, you will see Paul giving the same warning to the church at Corinth that I am giving to you today. He's referencing the golden calf story from Exodus here, and I know that we don't spend a lot of time in this day and age building golden statues in our garages, but, as we read this passage, try to think about the things in our lives that we put before

God..."

James replayed events from the previous night in his head. *If I could just watch her dance in that dress for the rest of my life, I'd be happy.* The entire congregation read from the Bibles in their laps. James's eyes wandered up near the stained glass windows. *There's got to be some way to change her mind. I was probably just being too forward. But what does she expect with a body like that?*

"...People make the mistake of thinking idol worship has to involve bowing down and singing songs to some inanimate object. When, in fact, you become an idol worshiper the moment you spend more time and energy on worldly things than you do your relationship with God, especially if you think those things will bring you happiness..."

James noticed a pretty brunette in a floral summer dress a few rows up and across the aisle. He had long debated with himself on the etiquette of checking out girls in church. Over the years, the internal argument swung in different directions, depending on the attractiveness of the girl. On one hand, only pure thoughts should enter one's mind in the house of God, right? But, on the other hand, God did make women incredibly beautiful for a reason.

James's attention bounced back and forth between the brunette and the idea of working the same shift as Ally that night. James feared the potential awkwardness, but held on to the slim hope that, if he apologized, he might be able to turn a negative situation into a positive. *As long as she's thinking about me, it's a good thing.*

"...In our culture today, we have turned to worshiping ourselves. We have become our own idols. If you look at social media and cell phones and iPods and advertisements, nearly everything is trying to capitalize off of our own self-interest. 'Do what you want to do, when you want to do it.' And in the act of regularly submitting to these impulses, we please Satan as we drift away from God. Perhaps the author of Jonah said it best, 'those who pay regard to vain idols forsake their hope of steadfast love.' Let us pray..."

While walking out of the church, James spotted the pretty brunette. The sun shone on her in such a way that the outline of her body could vaguely be seen through her dress. *Man, I should come to this church more often,* James thought, disregarding the fact that she held the hand of the man next to her, which concealed her wedding ring.

James rehearsed lines he wanted to say to Ally in his bathroom mirror before he left for Un Monde Parfait. After finishing the last of his Old Fitzgerald bourbon, which made him feel more convincing, James tucked in his shirt and headed out the door.

James clocked in at 5:05pm, not surprised by the restaurant's scant occupancy.

"Hey, man!" Tony said in his boisterous voice. "What happened to you last night?"

"It was kind of a crazy night. I ended up going home fairly early," James replied, scanning the restaurant floor as he answered.

"Alone?"

"Unfortunately, yeah."

"That's a bummer, bro. Well, there were a lotta girls at Aidan's."

"Oh yeah, what kind?"

"The kind that like guys like us."

"And what does that mean?"

"Stiff drinks and loose morals, maybe some tattoos and cigarettes."

"I see. I've spent many-a-night in bars like that."

"Then you know how awesome it is."

"I suppose I do," James said, unconvinced.

"Well, Dan is somewhere around here, so we better pretend to do some work. When he leaves, I'll come grab you for a break, okay?"

"Sounds good. Hey, one more thing—"

"Yeah?"

"When's Ally coming in?

"She already worked today."

"What?"

"Yeah, she switched shifts with Kevin and got out of here a few minutes ago. You just missed her. Why? What's up?"

"Oh, nothing."

"Okay, dude," Tony said with a smirk. "I'll see you in a bit."

James's mind couldn't help but drift throughout the majority of his shift, screwing up several orders in the process. Ranch became balsamic vinaigrette, Dr. Peppers became Diet Cokes, and vegetable medleys became garlic mashed potatoes. He couldn't stomach the idea of waiting another week to see Ally, anxious to atone for the previous night. However, James was not remorseful or apologetic. He viewed his error as one of bad timing and possibly a lack of grace. And it was in this mode of self-reflection (or self-absorption) that James failed to realize Ally's all-too-obvious reason for wanting to work earlier in the day.

It was well past 8:00pm before Tony was able to summon James. Business was slow, per usual for a Sunday evening, but people were lingering a bit longer than normal, persuaded by the summer sun to have one more drink.

"Come on," Tony motioned with his head, "Luis has got you covered." He was holding a liquor bottle in each hand.

"You sure?" James answered.

"Yeah, let's go."

Tony kicked open the back door before James could open it himself.

"What've you got there?"

"A bottle of Jack and this here's—Parker's Heritage." Tony turned the other bottle in order to read the label.

"I'll try that one," James said, pointing to the bottle of Parker's Heritage Bourbon.

"You would."

"What's that supposed to mean?"

"I'll get to that. But first, have a drink."

"Okay." James cracked the seal, unscrewed the cap, and took a sip. Tony tipped his head back for a long pull of Jack Daniels.

"How is it?" Tony asked as James dissected the layers of flavor.

"It's good. I'm trying to figure it out though. It's got a complex taste. Maybe it's one of those multi-grain whiskeys."

"Shit, you're talkin' over my head. I just pour the stuff and drink the stuff."

"It's definitely a rye, but it's got something else in

there too."

"Does knowing why it tastes good somehow make it taste better?"

"I don't know. I figure part of being a connoisseur is knowing what it's made of."

"Are you on a diet? Are you allergic to wheat? What does it matter?" Tony took another pull.

"Well, if I know the ingredients of one whiskey, or beer, I'll be able to predict whether I'll like others made from the same stuff. That way I'm hardly ever disappointed."

"Are you afraid of liking something you didn't expect to?"

"No. I just don't see the point in branching out if I already know what I like."

"You don't see that as limiting?"

"No. It's like the distilling process. You eliminate all the unwanted material in the quest for perfection of the final product. Speaking of which—" James took a slow sip.

"What if the distilling process is flawed?"

"Well, then I guess you'd consistently get something you didn't want. What's with all the questions anyway?"

"I'm an inquisitive guy," Tony said with a shrug and a smirk.

"But really, I can tell you're getting at something."

"Yeah, I guess I am."

"Well?"

"Let me ask you one more question."

"Okay."

"What's the one bad thing about having expensive taste?"

"It costs a lot of money?"

"Therefore?"

"You can't always get what you want?"

"Exactly!"

"Okay, I still don't follow. Wait, is this why you said 'you would' earlier?"

"Yeah. Well, sort of. Let me put it this way: why are you so interested in Ally?"

James choked on a mouthful of whiskey before answering, "What the fuck are you talking about? What does Ally have to do with anything?"

"We've been talking about her this whole time," Tony said calmly while lighting a cigarette.

"Did she tell you something happened?"

"No, but I think you just did."

"Fuck off! I told you I'm not that in to her."

"I didn't believe you then just like I don't believe you now."

"What are you, some kind of philosopher?"

"No, just an observant person."

James stared down at the pavement for a moment before speaking again.

"Why do you care anyway, Costa? Why is this any of your business?"

"I could pretend that I'm interested because you both work here, but I was under the impression that friends talked about stuff like this."

"Okay, fine. What do you want to know?"

"Answer my question, 'Why are you so interested in Ally'? Take a drink first, then answer the question."

"Okay." James obliged Tony by taking a long drink. "Alright, I'm interested in Ally because she's the hottest woman I've ever been around."

"Without a doubt. She's beautiful, which is to say, she tastes great, and I mean that figuratively, although it's probably literally true as well. Does that make sense?"

"I guess so."

"Allow me to clarify my analogy. Wait, is it an analogy or a metaphor?"

"They're basically the same thing."

"Alright. In this case, you have expensive taste. Ally is beautiful, she has 'a beautiful label', she's 'expensive', she's 'made by a reputable company'," Tony accompanied these statements with air quotes, although difficult to perceive with a cigarette in one hand and a bottle in the other. "But do you even know why you like her? Or in the words of the connoisseur, 'what she is made of'?"

James looked up at the clouds starting to turn an orangey-pink.

"Maybe that's a tough question," Tony interjected. "But let me say this: maybe you don't have the money to buy this bottle, and maybe that's a raw deal, but you do have the money to buy about everything else on the menu, like my friend Jack here." Tony took a pull. "Jack is served at every bar, especially at bars for dudes like us."

Tony's statements hung in the air with the cigarette smoke for a moment.

"How do you not pay attention to a woman like Ally?" James asked, pointing his finger.

"Shit, when they're that hot, I treat 'em kind of like cute high school girls. You can look, but you better not touch. But believe me, I'm lookin'."

"Well," James stood up with a sigh. "I never thought I'd say this, but can I go back to work now?"

"Sure. I'll be in right after this cigarette. Just leave that bottle with me."

Monday

James sat in the cramped conference room waiting for Monday's staff meeting to begin. Most people around the table engaged in small talk. James tapped his pen on the blank notepad in front of him, wanting desperately to hurry through this meeting and the following one with Janet. James had written next to nothing since Friday and wasn't in the mood to invent elaborate excuses. He had hopes of using the Band-Aid approach: do it fast, get it over with.

James looked up as Tori walked through the door. This week her hair was bleached blond, almost platinum, and cut shorter: still very punk, with chaotic strands of hair scattered in defiance of convention. *I almost forgot about her. But, how could I?*

The staff meeting went as usual. Tori made eye contact with James, but only once or twice.

James's meeting with Janet, however, was a little less than usual. First of all, James had to deal with the awkwardness of Tori and Brian's presence. Tori, because this was essentially the first time they had seen each other since she stuck her tongue down his throat and then vanished. And Brian, because James detested Brian, fearing, however irrationally, that Brian somehow knew about Tori and him. On top of that, James had to minimize Janet's frustration as he told her that there wasn't anything for her to read.

"I had a great interview with Cynthia. I got lots of good material. I just wasn't able to draft anything of consequence over the weekend—seeing as how I didn't meet with her until Saturday," James said.

"Well, I understand all of that, but don't form the habit of making excuses. I expect to read something on Mondays. Period," Janet said.

"I get that. I totally agree. Can I show you something by the end of the day?"

"Yeah, do that. But your whole column shouldn't depend solely on Cynthia. I still don't understand why you couldn't write the bulk of it without her."

"Let's just say she inspired me."

"Okay, whatever. I'll talk to you again after lunch then," Janet replied, short of patience and unsusceptible to sentimentality. "Tori, what have you got this week?"

"Well, I was trying to discuss the role of the full-length studio album in our ever growing, download friendly, commercial America. Here's what I have."

"Ah yes, that sounds very interesting," Janet said as she accepted Tori's hard copy.

James had to admit that it was an intriguing idea, but as usual, his mind drifted during this portion of the meeting. The last thing he heard was Janet saying, "...but do you think this has an appeal to the majority of our readership? That's my only concern..."

After the meeting, James went to his desk to work, keeping his thoughts to himself until noon. In that time, he was able to compose a very rough draft before heading out the door for lunch. Greeted by the midday sun, James decided to walk to a nearby bar for lunch. *A drink sounds good about now.*

Arbor Valley's downtown felt desolate: a sort of urban ghost town. Traffic was a dull whisper. James felt warm as he walked past the granite bricks of aging buildings, sunning themselves. A few blocks north of Columbia Avenue, James turned into a pub called Charlie's.

The place was empty except for a man in the far corner who was rearranging pool cues when James interrupted him.

"Are you guys open?"

"You bet. Go ahead and have a seat. I'll be right over."

James sat at the bar and looked out the large windows facing the street.

"Sorry about that," the man said after walking the length of the bar. "What would you like?"

"Are you guys serving food yet?"

"Yeah, it might take a bit longer. We're just gettin' everything back there fired up."

"That's fine. I'm not in a rush."

"Day off?"

"Not quite."

"Do you need a menu?"

"I'll just have a bacon burger if you've got one."

"Comes with BBQ sauce."

"That's fine."

"How do you like it?"

"Well done."

"Anything to drink?"

"I'll have a Full Sail," James said, pointing to the tap

handle.

"The pale?"

"Yeah."

"You've got good taste," the bartender said while placing a glass under the tap. "People who come here don't usually drink this kind of beer. It's not our crowd, I guess."

"Well, I'm happy to give you a change of pace then." *Is this guy going to lecture me too?*

"Here you go," he said, spinning around. "I'll go get your burger goin'."

"Thanks."

As James placed the cold glass to his lips, his gaze shifted back to the window. In the middle of a long sip, James had to double take as Tori walked past the window, looking right in at him. *What the hell?*

James swiveled in his bar stool as she walked in.

"Are you following me?" James asked.

"Don't be so paranoid," Tori said as she walked up to the bar. She wore an unbuttoned blue and white flannel over t-shirt and jeans.

"It's not paranoia if it's true."

"Is drinking at noon part of your normal Monday routine?"

"It is today."

"That's charming," she said sarcastically.

"Why don't you sit down? Let me buy you a drink."

"No, thanks. Not yet."

"Not yet?" James asked with raised eyebrows.

"Yeah, not yet," Tori said as she studied the array of bottles lining the bar.

"Well, then when?"

"Tonight. You can buy me a drink tonight."

"Oh yeah?" James chuckled. "I don't tend to go out on dates with people who tend to disappear without warning."

"Who said it was a date?

James smiled and sipped his beer. "Do you even remember going to the concert last week?"

"I remember most things."

Just then the bartender reemerged from the kitchen.

"Oh, I didn't know you had company. What can I get you?"

"Nothing. I'm fine, thanks," Tori replied.

"Alright, give me a holler if you need anything," the bartender said, then walked away.

"You don't want to join me for lunch?"

"No, I'm going to go now," she said pushing her sleeves up to her elbows. "I'll see you tonight."

"Oh yeah?"

"Yeah. Meet me at The Basement Bar at 9:00."

James said, "Alright," to her back as she began to walk out.

"That is—" she paused and turned at the doorway, "if you think you can keep up." And, with that, she left without giving a second glance. *What is this chick's deal?*

Minutes later the bartender returned with James's food.

"What'd you do? Scare her off already?"

"Yeah, something like that."

"Well, she's probably trouble anyway. Here you go," he said, setting down the food. "You want another beer?"

"Yeah."

"Same kind?"

"Yeah."

After a third beer and a purchase of gum, James returned to work. Minutes after doing so, he knocked on Janet's office door.

"Come in."

"Hey, Janet."

"What were you able to put together?"

"I think this is a fairly complete, yet very rough, draft," James said, handing over his hard copy. As resourceful and 'green' as Janet was, James knew that one of her obsessive-compulsive characteristics was her detest for reading things from computer screens when it wasn't necessary. It was probably her aging eyes, but she professed to some esoteric belief that words written on paper were somehow a more pristine expression.

"I think you're right. This is very rough," she said after reading all one thousand words, "but you always seem to pull through in these situations, so—" she cut herself off as she handed the document back.

"Thanks. And don't worry, I will."

James walked back to his desk, looking over his shoulder in Tori's direction. She didn't look up.

The Basement Bar had been the smokiest establishment in Arbor Valley until the smoking ban. James hadn't been there in years, and he wondered how loyal the clientele would be to a bar that had essentially lost its only charm. The cement stairs descending to the front door made you feel like you were going to Cheers, but nobody inside knew James's name, and for good reason. The Base-ment Bar attracted a blue-collar crowd that exchanged gruff discourse to which James could not relate. Anecdotes involving camping trips and gun collections, rodeos and ex-wives, pickup trucks and fist fights possessed a jovial camaraderie that existed only among men who labored for a living and enjoyed the company of those made from a similar mold.

When James walked through the doors at 8:35pm, to get one drink in before dealing with Tori's erratic behavior, he immediately asked himself the question: *why on earth did she bring me here*?

James took a seat at the bar as a barrel-chested bartender said, "Howdy, stranger!" through a mustache concealing his whole upper lip. "What'll you have?"

"What are the whiskey choices?" James answered.

"We have Evan Williams, Jack, and Jim."

"I'll have a Stone IPA, I guess," James said as he recognized the handle. *I might as well stick with beer.*

"Comin' right up."

As he waited for his drink, James surveyed the room. He noticed the Dale Earnhardt Jr. Budweiser hood hung proudly on the far wall. Almost every other inch of wall space was littered with dated sports memorabilia, including jerseys, pennants, and helmets. The patrons crowded around pitchers of cheap beer and slapped the table at every joke's crescendo. They hardly noticed James's presence.

"You need anything else?" the bartender asked, setting the beer down in front of him.

"No, thanks. Can you keep this open?" James said, handing him his debit card.

"Sure thing."

At 8:54pm James ordered a second beer to make it look like his first. And, at this time, he began regularly checking his phone for the time. A man who had recently sat down next to James seemed to notice his tick.

"Waitin' for someone?" he said.

"Yeah," James answered hesitantly. "Some girl from my work."

"Ooh, an office romance, huh?"

"Something like that, I guess."

"Sorry, let me introduce myself. My name is Greg Randolph. My friends call me Rando."

"I'm James, nice to meet you," he said, shaking hands.

"Say, a woman worth waiting for is something special. Assuming she's worth waiting for."

"Oh yeah?"

"Yeah. Take me and my wife for example. She refused to marry me until she was done with college. Four long years I waited. I knew if she wanted to go to college she was probably too good for me, so I figured I better not let this one go."

"So, she was worth it?"

"Shit yeah! I mean, I do get the earliest tee time I can every morning, now that I'm retired, so that I can get out of the house. But I still love the hell out of her."

"Well, you're a lucky man."

"Honestly, I don't think 'lucky's' the right word for it. It's got more to do with knowin' when to pull the trigger."

"Oh—"

"And who you're aimin' at."

"I see."

"Well, I'll go back to mindin' my own business. Good talkin' with ya, James."

"Yeah, likewise," James said as they shook hands again.

At 9:23pm James started to become a little wary. He ordered a third beer and said to himself: *this is it*. Rando patted him on the back on his way out. "Hang in there, James. It was nice to meet ya."

James was trying to stretch the last few ounces of beer in his glass at 10:15pm when he decided to cut his losses and go home. Before he could summon the bartender for his bill, he heard the door open behind him; he decided once more to turn around and see who it was. Tori walked through the door in a black cowl neck top and white skinny jeans. She looked unusually refined.

"Where the hell have you been?" James asked casually.

"Why? What time is it?" Tori asked as she paused to look through her wristlet.

Meanwhile the bartender noticed the newcomer. "What'll you have, miss?"

"Two Gimlets please," she said.

"No, thanks. I'm just having beer," James replied.

"Nonsense. If I'm going to let you buy me a drink, you're going to have to have one of these with me."

"So, two Giblets?" the bartender asked, waiting for the final verdict.

"Yes, please," Tori answered. "Now, let me slip in here," she said as she wedged herself between James and the barstool next to him, putting her hand on his upper thigh as she hoisted herself into position.

"I thought you weren't going to show up," James said.

"Were you worried?" she answered back with a grin.

"No, not exactly," James chuckled. "More curious than anything."

"Oh!" Her eyes lit up as she clapped her hands. "Here are our drinks."

"Just put 'em on my tab," James instructed the bartender. *Is this even the same woman?*

"Will do."

"What's in here exactly?" James asked Tori as he turned towards her in his seat.

"Gin and lime juice. But don't think, just drink." And with that, Tori clinked her shot glass against James' and drank it all down with one tilt of the head. James followed suit, almost involuntarily.

"Wow!" James said.

"It's good, huh?" she said, her smoky eyes looking sultry as they stared straight into James's.

"Yeah, it's not bad."

"Let's get two more then."

"You're crazy."

"I have the feeling you like that a little bit."

"I do like your hair."

"You do? You don't think it's too short?"

"No, it looks good. The sort-of-messy look works for you."

"If it was any shorter, it might end up looking like yours," Tori ran her fingers through James's hair as she said this, but pulled it back when she saw the bartender approach out of the corner of her eye. "Can we have two more, please?"

"Sure thing," the bartender answered.

"I told you you'd have to keep up."

"And I believed you when you said it. Remember, I've seen you in action before," James said, referring to the concert.

"Oh, that's right," Tori laughed, "I almost forgot."

"I thought you remembered most things."

"Did I say that?"

"Yep, you did. Today in fact."

"Well, I do and I don't."

The bartender interrupted with their new drinks. "Here you are."

"Thank you," they both said.

"Now you ready for round two?" Tori asked as she reached for her shot.

"I think so."

"Then, cheers!"

"Cheers," James echoed hastily, trying to keep up. He forced his head back, and when he lowered it again, Tori was already looking at him.

"Can I say something else?" she asked.

"Yeah."

"Come here," she said softly as she motioned him near with her finger.

James leaned forward and the words felt warm in his ear.

"I want you to fuck me."

James fumbled with his keys as he unlocked the apartment door. Tori clung tight to his shirt. Once inside, James stepped towards the kitchen counter to empty his pockets and felt her let go. When he turned, Tori was staring right through him. What faint light there was split her into two halves. The warm orange glow from the entry way acted as a diffused spotlight on one side; pale blue moon light washed over her other side, spilling through-out the entire living room.

Tori stepped back, out of the orange light, edging closer to the arm of the couch.

"Leave the lights off and come here," she said as her fingers reached from the blue light into the orange and motioned him close. Alcohol numbed the quickening thump within James's chest as he moved near.

"I like you like this," he said softly.

"Oh yeah?" she answered, pulling his face closer to hers with two handfuls of his shirt. He placed his hand at the small of her back as they kissed. "You have no idea," she said pulling back, as their eyes flitted between one another's. James then leaned in and they began to kiss more forcefully. James moved his hands to her waist, pressing it into his. He then slid his hands under her shirt, feeling the smooth skin of her sides, and pulled it up over her head. She ran one hand through James's hair, holding his head as she kissed him hard. He worked the clasp of her bra and eased her back against the couch. Her arms dropped to discard the bra; then he hoisted her onto the arm of the couch, fingers firm in the grooves between her ribs. She spread her legs, pulled him close and moved her hands up his bare back, helping guide the shirt over his head. James leaned forward and began kissing her neck. She tilted her head to the side and moaned softly.

"Lick my nipples," she said between breaths as she guided his head with her hands. James did so, placing his hands at the center of her arching back. "Harder," she said. James flicked his tongue and moved one hand down to start unbuttoning her pants. She interrupted him to say, "Here, let me do it." She pushed him back by the shoulders, stood up, and briskly wriggled her white jeans to the floor. Kicking them to the side, she said, "Come here," as she grabbed his belt, flung it open, and unzipped his pants. Then she turned around and leaned over the edge of the couch.

"Now fuck me." James pulled off her panties and grabbed her hips. Tori reached back to help guide him inside.

"Like this?" he asked.

"Yeah—yeah—yeah."

James continued to thrust, one hand tracing the outline of her leg, her ass, and her back in the coolness of the blue light, while the other firmly gripped her waist. Her body lacked the type of curves James was normally attracted to, but her frailness made James feel powerful.

As James started to quicken the pace, Tori craned her neck to glare back at him.

"Don't stop," she said.

James's eyes involuntarily closed as he felt himself finish.

"Keep going," Tori said with agitation. She dug her fingers into the arm of the couch and pushed back into him as she felt his grip loosen. James held onto her hips until he felt her go limp.

"Ah—that's better," she said, seemingly to herself, as she curled over the arm of the couch. James draped himself on top of her, but immediately felt that he was slipping out.

"I'll be right back," James said as he walked to his linen closet for a towel. When he came back, Tori had already slid all the way onto the couch. "Are you asleep?"

She replied with an inaudible groan. *Great, she's going to get it all over the cushions.* James then tried to scrunch the towel under her as best he could, but she grew stiff and unresponsive. *Fuck it!*

James retreated once more to the linen closet for a blanket. He returned to spread it over Tori and did his best to lie down beside her on the couch's remaining surface area.

"Good night."

Another, less audible, groan responded.

Tuesday

James woke up on his couch to find that he was alone. The sun was shining bright through the blinds James thought he had closed the night before. *That's funny.* His tongue smacked against the roof of his mouth, saturated by cheap gin; his stomach gurgled in objection to the mix of liquor and beer within it. *When the fuck did she leave?* James got up to check if Tori was in the bathroom. She wasn't. He then inspected the kitchen counter to see if she left a note. She didn't. *Do people even leave notes anymore?* Finally, James checked his bedroom, knowing full well she wouldn't be there. She wasn't. James walked to the center of his living room and stood there for a moment. *What the fuck?*

James walked through *Idyll's* office doors at 8:55am to begin what already felt like an unusual day. The typical awkwardness of waking up next to someone for the first time was compounded by the fact that he and Tori worked together. And that was compounded by the peculiarity of them not waking up next to each other at all.

The regularly early employees were there already,

including Rob, the local news writer; Scott, the chief writer and editor of sports and recreation; and Brian. James's eyes scanned Tori's cubicle, but found it unoccupied. James stopped to talk with Brian, of all people.

"Hey, Brian, have you seen Tori?"

"No, not yet. Why?"

"Oh, nothin'. I just thought I had a cool idea for her article," James said, improvising.

"Yeah, I think she's running a little late. Big surprise, huh?"

"Hm, Yeah," James tried to force a chuckle. "Well, I'll leave you alone. I know I've got plenty to do."

"No problem. And, James—" Brian said as James started to walk away.

"Yeah?"

"I meant to tell you that I truly enjoyed your piece last week. I thought it was really good," Brian said with genuine sincerity. "I have aunts and uncles who are teachers and professors. They would have appreciated your perspective."

"Thanks, Brian. That's very nice of you. Well, have a good rest of your morning."

"You too."

James sat down at his desk without giving much consideration to Brian's kind words. Instead, he forced himself to focus on his deadline as he struggled to revise his currently porous draft.

An hour later, Tori walked through the front doors, moving briskly, as if somewhat flustered, with a grey hoodie partially concealing the wires to her head phones.

She bypassed her own desk, gave James a curt "morning" without slowing down, and knocked on Janet's office door before uncovering her blond, disheveled hair. James failed to respond before he heard Janet's door open, followed by a faint "come on in."

When Janet's office door opened again, Tori walked out and went straight to her desk without saying anything to anyone. Having caught her blur in his peripheral vision, James leaned out into the aisle to watch Tori disappear behind her cubicle. Knowing that he couldn't 'play it cool' throughout the whole day, James said to himself, *I might as well get it over with*, and got up to go talk to her.

"Hey, how's it goin'?"

"Not bad," she said as she continued typing. "Just a little stressed." Her thumbs tapped the space bar through the pre-made holes in her sleeves.

"You want to grab a smoke?"

"I thought you didn't smoke," she said, finally turning to look at him.

"I don't." *Don't play dumb.* "You know what I mean, though."

"I can't right now. I just got in. I can't take a break yet. Plus, I really want to impress Janet with this piece. I better keep working."

"Alright, I'll leave you alone. Just let me know when you're takin' a break."

"Okay," she answered. Her eyes already back to her computer screen.

After frequent checks of his watch, even though the time was clearly displayed on his computer screen, and diminutive progress made on his final draft, James got tired of waiting for Tori and approached her desk once more.

"How 'bout now?" James asked with both palms to the sky.

"Alright," Tori exhaled. "I guess I could pause here."

"Good."

"You're pretty eager to take breaks for a guy who hardly had anything to show Janet yesterday."

"I've been doin' this for a while."

"Have you? I'm thinkin' you must have been inspired," she said through a slight curve of a smile. "Let's go," she said, snatching her bag from the floor.

The sun was warm but muted by a thin layer of clouds. Once seated on her customary curb, Tori rummaged through her khaki colored bag in search of cigarettes.

"What were you talking to Janet about?" James asked.

"I had to tell her where I was."

"Which was?"

"I stopped by Turntable Records," she paused to light a cigarette, "to interview their manager about my article."

"This late?"

"Yeah. He was impossible to get a hold of all last week. It seems like no one checks voicemail anymore."

"Was he helpful?"

"Yeah. I just needed some current sales trends. Stuff like that. We'll see if I even keep it in there."

A silence ensued as James pondered how to change the subject. *I better just say it.* Tori toed a pebble along the asphalt in between drags.

"So where were you this morning?"

"What do you mean?"

"I mean, when I woke up this morning you were gone."

"So, yeah, what's your point?"

"Uh, I don't know. I just wanted to make sure nothin' was wrong."

"No, nothing's wrong."

"Okay. Never mind."

"Listen to you," Tori said with a laugh. "You act like you've never fucked before."

"Now wait a minute. It's got nothin' to do with that. I've been with plenty of girls before," James said defensively. *Ah, that makes me sound like such a douche.*

"You may have had sex with plenty of girls. You might have even made love a few times. But that doesn't mean you've fucked." Tori took a drag and exhaled to the side with self-assured coolness.

"I didn't know this was a lesson in semantics."

"Call it what you want. But I wanted to shower and get dressed at my own place this morning. Is that so crazy?"

"No."

"Sounds like a pretty reasonable way to start a workday to me." And with that, Tori twisted her cigarette butt into the concrete curb and got up to go inside.

Why am I even worried about this chick?

Wednesday

Most of Wednesday was uneventful. James spoke with no one beyond the typical salutations. His only goal was to leave work that day with a solid idea of what he was writing about for the following week, seeing as though he would be gone Thursday and Friday for his interview in Seattle. He had dismissed several ideas, including the average American's shocking lack of fear displayed towards the growing threat of North Korean hostility, the tangible effects that handheld devices and social media have had on interpersonal communication, and an analysis of the extent to which ignorance feeds the public's continuing distrust of government. By early afternoon, James had settled on a discussion about the moral obligation of paying taxes: a cry for civic duty. To avoid an immense constitutional debate, James decided to focus only on how the issue comes to fruition in Arbor Valley's more intimate community. Not long after that, Janet called James back to her office.

"Come on in, James. I wanted to talk to you before you left today," Janet said with a wave of her hand.

"Alright," James said before he closed the door behind him.

"Please, take a seat."

"Thanks."

"I want you to think about something for me while you're off to Seattle," she said, adjusting herself in her chair.

"Okay, I can do that."

"As you know, Brian and Tori are here on sort of a trial basis."

James nodded.

"And that trial is coming to an end. See, we hired them at the beginning of the year and now it's time to decide who to keep. Who's worth keeping, that is."

"I see. So where do I fit in?"

"Well, this decision would be tough for me in general, because I feel that both of them are legitimately qualified and/or talented. But the decision is further complicated by the fact that I know Brian's family so well. Now, I know I shouldn't care about people's feeling so much, but in the interest of objectivity, you're going to make the decision for me. I know that if I picked Brian it would seem too biased."

"I'm making the decision?" James said with angst in his voice.

"Yes. Both Lauren and I trust your judgment, you've worked closely with both of them, and it might be a nice way to leave an imprint on this place if, in fact, you do leave, which would give us a whole 'nother problem to worry about."

"I don't know if I feel comfortable with this."

"I appreciate your sentiment, but we've decided to do it this way. Brian and Tori already know who's making the decision and—"

"Wait! Brian and Tori know?" *Holy fucking shit!*

"Yes." Janet answered, sitting forward in a slightly defensive posture. "In the pursuit of full transparency, I thought it was only fair that they knew who was judging them."

"How long have they known?" James asked, fearing what he thought he already knew.

"I think I told them the week before last. Why? What does it matter?"

"I don't know. I guess I feel kind of out of the loop," James said, fighting a sudden torrent of the mind.

"Well, I probably should have told you sooner. That's my fault. But my plan was for you to choose intuitively. I didn't want you over-thinking it. You know, looking for things that weren't there. Plus, I didn't want it to be a distraction for you."

She's giving herself way too much credit here. "Okay," James said dispassionately.

"The bottom line is that I'd like for you to tell me on Monday who you think would make a better fit for the paper. Can you do that for me?"

"Yeah, I guess I can."

"Good," Janet said as she stood to shake on the deal. "You know, James, before too long it's going to be your job to make decisions like this."

"I can't wait," James said with a rigid smile as he turned to leave.

"Good luck in Seattle, James."

"Thanks," he said over his shoulder.

"Try to enjoy it."

James sat as his desk processing information for almost an hour, mulling over sequences of events. He struggled to remain calm as he pieced together the tremendously obvious. James had felt that Tori's sudden interest in him was peculiar from the get-go, but now Janet's news made the situation painfully clear.

Did she really plan this all out?

James tried to rationalize the possibility of coincidence because, in his mind, it wasn't out of the question for Tori to throw herself at him. But a sting of embarrassment began to wash away denial and left him pondering the worst-case scenario.

Or is she just a slut?

The only issue left for debate was whether or not to confront her on the matter. James prided himself on being a truly rational person, so he convinced himself there would be nothing to gain by calling her out at the office. Fueled by emotions. In front of people. Where she'd naturally be defensive. He grew tired of thinking about it and felt that he could no longer be productive at work, so he decided to leave early. It was 1:30pm.

James stoically walked out of the office, avoiding all eye contact. Although his decision to leave without conflict was surely a wise one, what he failed to admit was that his clear, logical analysis was simply a justification for the fact that he was too ashamed to hear Tori tell him the truth.

What a crazy bitch.

On his way home, James stopped by the liquor store to pick up a bottle of Rittenhouse Straight Rye Whiskey. He figured packing for his trip to Seattle would be the best way to get work off his mind, and James found mixing chores, or any manual labor, with alcohol to be a perfect marriage. The alcohol made the chores more enjoyable, and the labor made the drinking less irresponsible.

After a small duffel was full of Friday's clothes and some toiletries, James decided to make his weekly phone call to his mother, drink in hand.

"Hi, James, how are you?"

"I'm good, mom, how are you doin'?"

"Can't complain. Just enjoying my afternoon off."

"That's good. So, I was just calling to let you know that I'm flying to Seattle tomorrow for a job interview."

"Ooh, that sounds exciting! What's it for?"

"It's a writing position for this magazine that highlights the Northwest lifestyle."

"That's great! It's about time you work for someone who'll make use of your talent."

"Yes, mom, we all agree," James said sarcastically. A trait his mother never appreciated.

"I'm serious. You're more talented than all those people you work with now."

"How do you know? You don't even live here now. You never read *Idyll*."

"I look at it online sometimes. And don't talk to me that way."

"Okay. Sorry."

"By the way, do you have a girlfriend yet? Or am I going to die before I have any grandchildren?" she asked, changing the subject quickly. These swift transitions were usual parts of their conversations.

"No, I don't have a girlfriend. But I promise you, you'll be the first to know when I do."

"I hope so. You know I'm beginning to worry about you."

"Why?"

"What do you mean 'why'? You're almost thirty and you haven't settled down yet. You don't even have your career figured out. How are you going to support a family?"

"I don't know. I guess it's just not a priority."

"Well, it should be."

"Have you ever considered the fact that you and I might have different plans for my life?"

"Oh yeah? What is your plan? Enlighten me."

"Uh—well, I am going to a job interview tomorrow," James said a bit defensively.

"I'm sorry. You know I just want what's best for you."

"I know. You and every other mother."

"I'm serious. You can do anything you put your mind to. You're talented. You're handsome. You're—"

"Okay, mom. I got it. I appreciate what you're saying. Just try to not make such a big deal out of everything."

"Are you still going to church?" she asked without even trying to transition smoothly.

"Yes, mom."

"And what have they been saying?"

"The same thing they've been saying for years."

"Being close minded won't help anything, James."

"Okay. I called to say I was leaving town for a couple of days. I think we've had enough lecturing for today."

"Alright. But if you don't take my advice, hopefully you're listening to someone else's. It can be scary figuring everything out on your own."

"You're probably right."

"Well, have fun on your trip. Knock 'em dead in the interview."

"Thanks, I will."

"Good bye, James."

"Bye, mom." And with that, James finished his drink and decided to text Tony.

"Do you want to get drunk tonight?"

James turned the TV on as he waited for a response from Tony. He soon realized that only housewives, deadbeats, and little kids were supposed to be home at 4:07pm. He turned off the TV and got up to choose some music when an idea struck him. *Tori knew I was making the decision. But did she know that I didn't know? Does that change anything? Would that make her more or less scandalous?*

James jostled with these thoughts as he began to contemplate his decision for the first time. In Janet's office he was in shock. Now he could try thinking about who he was going to choose. *I'm definitely not going to be objective on this one.*

James selected a Violent Femmes hits album and started it on "Gimme The Car." After pouring himself another drink, James sat back down in his recliner.

Eventually, Tony wrote back, "working til close u up for meeting after".

James replied, "I better pass. Got to fly to Seattle tomorrow morning."

"ok we'll be at Aidens. Text if u change ur mind"

James considered calling Cade, but thought it wasn't a worthwhile endeavor on a Wednesday night. Once the album circled back to track 6, James got up and carved a similarly shaped path as he turned off the music, retrieved the Rittenhouse from the counter, and plopped back down in the recliner. He set the bottle down on the end table and eyed his journal for a moment. *Hmm.*

Maybe more than one woman wants him when he's rich. James filled his glass nearly to the brim. *Maybe he could have both.* He snorted a small laugh before muttering, "Two chicks at the same time" in a gruff voice. *Nah, I'd have to change too much,* he thought as he gently extended the footrest so as not to spill his drink. James turned the TV back on, flipping back and forth between movie channels for hours trying to catch a glimpse of nudity.

James woke up in his recliner at 1:03am, having sipped his way through half the bottle of whiskey, and headed to bed for a few more hours of sleep.

Thursday

James's plane landed at 8:55am, almost the exact time that it took off. As the plane taxied, James checked his phone to see if it had yet switched to Pacific Time. He left his watch on Mountain Time, a usual custom whenever he traveled.

Outside the Sea-Tac Airport, James hopped on the metro and took it north towards Lake Union. He accidentally got off a station too early and had to walk the remaining blocks to the Residence Inn near Lake Union Park. There, he was able to check into his room early and change for his interview at noon. James put on his best pair of tan slacks, a royal blue dress shirt he'd had since high school, and a silver and blue tie. While adjusting his tie in the mirror, James realized that his mother had purchased all the clothes he was wearing. *I seriously need to update my wardrobe.*

After eating a small breakfast and clarifying directions with the hotel staff, James decided to walk the several blocks to the interview. He still had plenty of time, and he thought the mild exercise and fresh, coastal air would help combat his nerves.

Walking down Fairview Ave, James could see the

Space Needle off to his right. The iconic beauty of its structure contrasted greatly with the rust colored hulk of the public storage unit that he currently walked past. In front of him lay taller buildings at the northern edge of Seattle's downtown, one of which was his destination. Cranes signaled the beginning of summer construction projects, and the dull roar of jackhammers in the distance gave James the sensation of living a true urban experience.

At the next crosswalk, James shifted the strap of his work bag, a gift from his mother when he began working at *Idyll*, to avoid getting an embarrassing sweat mark across his shoulder. When the sign changed to 'walk', James hesitated to make sure the traffic came to a halt. As he began crossing the intersection, he noticed a city bus with an advertisement for the *Northwest Metropolitan* running along its side. *Wow! I gotta get this job.*

James sat in the foyer for thirty minutes before Jack Wheaton opened the door and said, "Hey, James, come on in." He held the door open and extended his hand. "It's a pleasure to meet you, and thanks for coming all this way to see us."

"It's nice to meet you too," James said as they shook hands.

"We're going to be straight back and on the right there."

"Alright."

Jack Wheaton had dark hair that had silvered at the temples, the slender build of a runner, and fine features that made him look younger than his forty-five years. He made quick conversation, like someone trying to stay on schedule, yet maintained a sincerity that made you feel that he was genuine.

"Go ahead and have a seat there," Jack said as they reached his office.

"Okay, thanks," James said, sitting in front of the large wooden desk.

"Can I offer you anything to drink? A latte? Coffee? Some water?"

"No, I'm fine. Thanks."

"Are you sure?"

"I guess some coffee would be nice."

"Stacy, can you get James a coffee, please? Thanks," he called to his assistant.

"Wow, your view is amazing," James said, looking out over several city blocks that led down to Pike Place Market and opened up into Puget Sound.

"Yeah, that's one of the perks of being up here. It's a beautiful day today too." Jack made his way to the window as he spoke. "Sometimes, when it's cloudy, you can hardly make out the water. Today, you can see way out there." He then took a seat at his desk.

"Well, it's impressive."

Jack smiled in reply. "Shall we get started? Oh, here's your coffee."

Stacy walked in and set James's coffee down on the desk. She was young and wore a sky-blue blouse with a dark grey pencil skirt.

"Here you are," she said.

"Thank you," James replied. *I wish I could turn to watch her leave.* Her perfume lingered momentarily.

"Now, let's get started," Jack said.

"Sounds good," James answered with a confident nod.

"James, where do you see yourself in ten years?"

"Uh—well, I'd like to be working for a good company like this one. Writing in some capacity. Continuing to work my way up."

"Let me ask the same question in a slightly different way: Where do you see your self in ten years?" Jack said, separating 'your' from 'self'.

"Oh, I see," James said, eyes scanning the room in thought. "To be honest, I'd like to have had a novel published by then. I'd like to make a big enough splash to be able to have my work sustain me. I'd like to hone my craft to the degree that I felt like I had an absolutely clear vision of what I wanted to do with my work. And in that sense, my life." James regained eye contact as he answered.

"Interesting. Any family in that picture?"

"Not right now. Of course, I'd probably like to have a family and all that ten years from now, but I sort of want to find my way and have everything figured out before I make that commitment." James noticed Jack's array of family photos on his desk. Wife, two daughters, and a son. All smiling. "But believe me, my mom sure wants me to get going on the family front."

"Ah, yes," Jack smiled. "Mothers are good for that. Mothers-in-law are even better."

"I bet."

"Now, why do you think you're drawn to writing, as a career?"

"Well, I like to tell stories. I guess that's the simplest answer. But—" James took note of the areca palm silk plants and the Chinese evergreens stationed on the corner bookshelves and filing cabinets made of mahogany and cherry wood. "—the act of dispensing knowledge may be the most enjoyable part. Giving people insights that they find valuable. I think that the best thing our writing can do for people is to get them to think about something they may never have thought of if it wasn't for us."

"I like that answer."

"That, and I'm good at it. I tend to stick to things I'm good at." *Don't sound limited.*

"Well, at least you know what you're good at, right?"

"I'd like to think so."

"If you had to identify your greatest weakness, what would you say that is?"

"Wow." James's eyes drifted to the walls. They were littered with the usual certificates, the first issues of magazines, and prints of various paintings. All sentimentally framed. "I'd say that I do a good job at *Idyll.* And sometimes, when you do a good job and people are telling you you're doing a good job, you can get a bit complacent. I've grown pretty accustomed to my role there, and that's why I'm so excited for this new challenge. I think it will allow me to create my best work to date."

"Can you describe how you feel about working as part of a team?"

"Sure." *I'll have to BS this one a bit.* "I think anyone who is honest eventually realizes that any success in the professional world is team success. There's never one person who does all the work. It takes many moving parts to make the whole thing work. As far as working on a particular project, I've learned to just look at the positives. Instead of fearing the loss of creative control, or something, I focus on the fact that everyone in the group brings something different to the table." As James took a sip of coffee, his eyes were drawn to a painting with a blue background.

"In a group setting, what would you say you 'bring to the table'?" Jack asked, bringing James's eyes back to him.

"I think I'm calm, first of all. I don't get too up, and I don't get too down. I'm organized. I know how to prioritize. And I think I give people enough space to do their job well." James crossed his right leg over his left, turning his body slightly towards the blue painting.

"How do you feel about deadlines?"

"Well, I suppose it's a little bit of a love-hate relationship." In the painting, a man and woman embrace inside what looks like the trunk of a tree. They're naked, and their faces are concealed. "Deadlines always cause stress, which is natural, but I've always appreciated deadlines. Nothing helps you get more done. I always write best with a deadline looming."

"That's good to hear because we certainly have to be strict about deadlines. Our process for publication is a little more time consuming than you're used to, so you'll probably have a smaller window in which to work."

"Okay, no problem."

"Now you may not have a full understanding of our market, but this position entails writing about the nightlife in the Northwest. You'll be visiting restaurants, bars, and clubs. I want you to tell me what your future readers want to hear."

"Well, I think one thing everyone wants is a new experience. And because of that, you have to treat every establishment as an individual character." The man is painted dark blue while the woman has a realistic, healthy, Caucasian skin tone, accented by auburn colored hair. "If each establishment is a character, then my goal would be to isolate, and possibly exaggerate, whatever made that place feel unique. People want to go somewhere that will give them a special experience, has a certain vibe, so I would have to make every place feel special. That way, you're doing justice to the proprietor and the reader/potential customer." The man's torso seems to be pulling away from the woman, yet his head is turned over his left shoulder to kiss her. *She reminds me of Amber.*

"I see," Jack paused as if mulling over some details. "Well, that concludes this portion of the interview. I'll go over your work samples and show you around the office in a second. But first, do you have any questions for me?"

"Yeah, I actually have kind of an odd one."

"Okay."

"Can you tell me who painted that?"

"The one with the blue background?"

"Yeah."

"It's a Max Ernst painting. Pretty interesting, huh?"

"Ernst. I swear I've heard that before."

"He was a surrealist painter in the early twentieth century."

No, like recently. "Do you know the name of it?"

"I believe the actual title is in French, but it translates to something like *Long Live Love*. It's also called *The Charming Countryside*, but I don't like that as much. It seems to miss the point."

"I agree. But it does seem like a strange depiction of love."

"I think you're right about that. Well, why don't you

grab a few of your work samples and I'll show you around a bit."

"Alright." James rummaged through his work bag to find a few hard copies of *Idyll*. "I have electronic versions of these too, if you prefer."

"That's fine. I'll get those from you when we come back. Just set those there for now. Thanks," Jack said as he stood up from his desk. "Shall we take a walk?"

"Sounds good to me," James answered and got up to follow Jack out the door.

"Right this way."

James took one more glance at the painting as they started down the hall. In the foreground, an internal organ seems to be waving goodbye to the couple.

Having searched for the nearest restaurants and bars, James enjoyed a great seafood dinner at Chandlers 0.1 miles away, and then took a stroll south 0.4 miles to Brave Horse Tavern for drinks before walking back to the hotel. He spent much of the afternoon in downtown Seattle and enjoyed it, but by evening he had sought the quietness and solitude of a night alone. He felt strangely, although not in a bad way. He couldn't quite put his finger on it, but he'd felt it ever since leaving the interview.

James entered his room at 10:53pm. He kicked off his shoes and sat on the bed to watch ESPN. It didn't take long for him to feel inundated by the monotony of baseball highlights. So, after sifting through the remaining channels, James decided to hit the 'menu' button and scroll over to the 'adult entertainment' tab. Before carefully surveying the options, James scampered over to the room's mini fridge, broke the seal, and ran his fingers across the labels of the tiny liquor bottles inside. Jack Daniels and Jim Beam were the only available whiskeys. *These will be perfect.*

James resituated several pillows for optimum comfort and then assumed a reclined position on the bed. He cracked open the 50ml bottle of Jack Daniels first and took a sip. *I could get used to this.*

The list of movies included *Anal Invaders*, a space motif; *Wet 'N Wild Weekend*, a beach house full of sexy coeds; *Hot Cop*, which sort of speaks for itself; and many other 'innovative' titles. Each movie displayed enticing cover art and a short blurb describing the plot. James could normally see himself laughing at these summaries, but this time he found himself examining each one with excessive care. *I've got to find the right one.*

James was equally dismissive of each imperfect option based on the images and the words alike. First, he critiqued the female protagonists: *I don't want any blondes. Too exotic. No gaudy blue eye shadow. I'm not in the mood for Asians. She's got a horrible fake tan. She's hot, but no. Her tits are too big.* Then the plots: *Who gets turned on by outer space? No dominatrix stuff. I want a little bit of a story. I don't want her to be that sassy.*

Finally, James settled on what he deemed the perfect choice. The blurb read:

"Unassuming beauty, Jane, finds herself to be the center of attention in her small town after she posts a personal ad seeking more 'experience' in response to her boyfriend dumping her for being 'too prude'. She's out to prove him wrong as she realizes her town isn't so small after all."

This particular movie was titled *Hometown Hottie*.

The star of this movie had reddish-light brown hair and fair skin. They dressed her down, at least to begin with, to appear very average. *She looks a lot like Amber*, James thought, as he finished the little bottle of Jack Daniels. *This is exactly what I want*.

James pushed play and accepted the $13.99 charge to the room.

Friday

James purposely scheduled a late afternoon flight on Friday so as to not be back in time for work, at either job. When he arrived at his apartment at 5:31pm, he quickly unpacked his things and prepared himself a drink from the half bottle of Rittenhouse he had left waiting for him. To get a better view of the way the evening sun cut shadows into the foothills, James dragged his recliner to the other side of the living room window and spun it around to face the opposite direction. Once James took a seat to appreciate the view, he noticed that the sun wasn't going to create the desired effect for several more hours. *Damn summer. I guess I'll just have to wait.* Then he spotted his journal on the end table and got up to retrieve it. *I think I finally have a good idea.* James sat back down in his chair, sipped his drink, and began to write.

When the sun was all the way down, and several pages were all the way filled, and the bottle of Rittenhouse was all the way empty, James drove to Amber's house.

She lived in what was considered the periphery of Arbor Valley in the 1960s but was now just considered a short drive from downtown. The homes were quaint and boasted ironically inefficient floor plans, but if one kept up their property and had any design sensibility, most guests thought of these homes as 'cozy' or 'cute' or 'retro'. James assumed Amber chose to live in this neighborhood because of the affordable rent.

As James walked up to the house, he noticed the flicker of the TV through the blinds. *Good, she's home.* James walked past a strange car in the driveway and knocked on the door. The muffled sound of the TV went silent as a shadow moved within the window to come unlock the door. Amber opened the door just wide enough to identify her visitor.

"Hi."

"What are you doing here?" Amber asked in a hushed voice.

"I needed to see you."

"Why didn't you call first?"

"I don't know. I guess I didn't think you would answer. I just need to talk to you in person."

"Well, now's not a good time."

"Can I just come in so we can talk?" James pleaded, leaning in close, with his hand on the door frame.

"You'll have to call me tomorrow."

"I don't think you under—" James pushed his way through the door and froze when he saw the guy sitting on Amber's couch, "—stand. Who's this?"

"That's Chris. That's my date."

"Oh."

"Chris, this is James," Amber introduced the two with disdain for the situation.

"Hey," Chris answered, echoing the sentiment.

"Hi," James said.

"He was just leaving; weren't you, James?" Amber added.

"I've got to talk to you first."

"James, you're being really rude. Are you drunk?"

"It'll just take a second, I swear."

"Ugh, fine," Amber sighed, gesturing with her hand for James to step back outside. James obliged. Amber embarrassingly apologized to Chris before pulling the door shut behind her.

"Now, what's so important that—"

"Listen," James said, cutting her off. "I've been seeing things differently lately. I know I haven't been fair to you at all, and I'm sorry for that. I truly am. I thought I knew what I wanted, what was good for me. But, it turns out that, you're what's good for me. I see that now. And I want to make it up to you."

"Where did all this come from?"

"I saw you in a painting and I—"

"You saw me in a painting?"

"Well, I didn't see you you. I saw a version of you."

"Huh? What are you talking about?"

"I saw someone who looked like you, who reminded me of you." Amber looked at him with impatient confusion. "Look, I was in a job interview in Seattle and there was this painting on the wall, and it caught my eye; I kind of thought the girl in the painting looked like you, but all that doesn't matter. All that matters is that I thought of you. It made me want to be with you."

"This all just sounds really weird."

"That's fine if it sounds weird. I'm just trying to be honest. Honest with you. Honest with myself."

"Honest, huh?"

"Yeah."

"Then where was all of this six months ago? Or last week?"

"Honestly, I don't know. I think I was selfish. I was arrogant." James noticed Amber's eyes roll. "But, you're not like that, and that's why I need you."

"Did you ever stop to think about whether I need you? About whether you're good for me?" Amber said with soft-spoken conviction.

James hesitated. "But, I—I think I love you."

"You're too late."

"Too late? But I said I'm sorry. I'm gonna be different now."

"I'm sure you will. Just not with me."

"Oh, so you're already in love with this guy?" James said, a bit agitated.

"He's got nothing to do with this," Amber aggressively asserted. "I'm not even having a good time," she said, trying to hold her voice to a whisper.

"I'm confused. You'd rather go on a date with a guy you don't even like?"

"Shhh. And yes, that is what I'm saying."

"I don't get it."

"You don't have to get it. You just have to know that sometimes it's better to be with someone you don't love than to be with someone you love who doesn't love you back."

"But that's what I'm tryin' to tell you. I do love you back."

"But you didn't."

James was left speechless as their eyes scanned each other's throughout an uncomfortable silence.

"I've got to get back inside. I'm being rude," Amber said abruptly.

"So, that's it?"

"I'm afraid so. Take care." And, with that, Amber stepped inside and closed the door.

What did I do wrong?

James staggered back to his car and sat in the driver's seat for nearly a half hour before putting the key into the ignition. *Why didn't it work?* He squeezed his eyes shut and gritted his teeth several times in frustration. When his eyes opened the final time, his vision was blurry.

Saturday

James was eating a turkey sandwich at 3:02pm when he called Un Monde Parfait.

"Un Monde Parfait, how may I help you?"

"Is Tony there yet?"

"Yes, I believe so."

"Can you put him on, please?"

"Yeah, it'll be just a moment."

"Thanks."

James took a bite of his sandwich while he waited.

"Hello, this is Tony."

"Hey, Costa, this is James."

"Hey, what's up? You're comin' today, right?"

"Yeah, don't worry. I'll be there."

"That's good. So, what do you need?"

"Is Ally working the early shift again?" James asked without hesitation.

"Oh, man! You just can't let her go, can you?" Tony laughed.

"Ha, ha. Just tell me. It'll be the last time I bug you about it."

"I don't know, dude."

"If she's there, I'll come in early and work."

"It's not that. It's just that she begged me <u>not</u> to tell you she was working until five today."

"Thanks, man. I owe you," James said with a grin. "And did she really tell you that?"

"You flatter yourself too much, man."

"She didn't say anything?"

"Nothing."

"Alright, I'll let you go."

"Later."

James clocked in at 4:06pm and waited near the kitchen for Ally to punch in her next order. *I don't think she saw me come in.* James watched her snake from table to table, progressively moving her way back to the kitchen until she was only a few feet away.

"Hey, Ally, can I talk to you for a second?" James asked.

"I'm busy. What is it?" Ally responded without stopping what she was doing.

"I don't mean to bother you at all. I just wondered if we could talk. Just for a moment."

"Well, now is obviously not a good time."

"How about when you clock off? I'll walk you out." She didn't respond as her fingers worked furiously at the digital screen of the POS. "Part of it's that I wanted a chance to apologize," James added.

"Listen, James," she said, finally making eye contact. "I don't mean to sound like a bitch or anything, but I don't think we should hang out anymore, especially alone."

"It's not like that. I understand," James said, putting his hands up to signify his innocence. "I just want to say a few things, as a friend."

"Fine."

"You're off at five?"

"Yeah."

"I'll meet you here."

"Okay," Ally said as she made her way to the bar.

At 5:01pm Ally clocked off and went into a back room to retrieve her things. When she walked back out onto the restaurant floor, James was waiting for her.

"Shall we?" James asked as he gestured towards the front entrance.

"Sure. But I'd hurry if I were you. Kyle's going to be here any minute to pick me up."

"No problem," James answered as they began walking. "So, you told him about last weekend?"

"Yeah, why?"

"What'd you tell him?" James held open the door for Ally. She waited to respond until they were outside.

"I told him you tried to kiss me," Ally said as she folded her arms.

"Was he mad?"

"Of course."

"Was he mad at you?"

"Yeah, a little." Ally cocked her head with interest. "Why do you ask?"

"Listen," James said as they stood on the sidewalk directly in front of Un Monde Parfait. "The first thing I want to do is apologize, something I'm not normally that good at. I'm genuinely sorry for making you feel uncomfortable, or encroaching on our friendship, or overstepping my bounds. But—"

"Ah, there's always a 'but'."

"Well, this is a pretty big 'but'. You have to realize that you're an extremely beautiful woman." Ally didn't break eye contact to blush. She stood expressionless and unsurprised. "That any sane guy would jump at the chance to go out with you. Let me ask you this: do you have any guy friends?"

"Yeah, I have lots of them."

"Are any of them gay?"

"A few."

"Well, the rest have a crush on you."

"Don't be ridiculous."

"I'm not. I don't think you fully understand guys."

"I don't?"

"No. No heterosexual man wants to be friends with an attractive woman unless he wants to sleep with her."

"You're full of it. I've had some guy friends for years."

"Some are willing to wait that long. It's a simple ratio. The more beautiful the girl is, the longer a guy will tolerate just being friends with her."

"Is this really what you wanted to talk to me about? I don't see your point," Ally said with frustration as she looked for her ride.

"My point is that I was just doing what every guy wants to do when I kissed you. I just had the guts to do it."

"If you want to call it that."

"That's why your boyfriend—"

"Kyle," Ally interjected.

"That's why Kyle was a little mad at you too. He knew that any guy in his right mind would make a move on you and couldn't be entirely to blame. He probably told you not to strut your stuff so much, not to tempt the leering men in all the bars out there."

"Are you saying it's my fault?"

"Partly," James said with a shrug.

"You have a funny way of apologizing."

"I'm sorry. I told you I wasn't very good at it."

"Well, if you want to ask Kyle about it, here he is," Ally said as Kyle pulled up to the curb in a silver late model Mustang. A graphic for his marketing company was splayed across the side. He got out of the car as soon as it came to a stop.

"Ally, is this the guy?" Kyle barked as he rounded the car in a navy blue dress shirt and gray suit pants. His blond hair was gelled into place, and you could tell he worked out his upper body far more than his lower half.

"Yeah, but we were just talking," Ally said.

"Hi, I'm James—" But before James could extend his hand, Kyle's fist landed right between his left cheek and the bridge of his nose. The impact forced James to step back, unfortunately into a tree well, causing him to fall flat on his back. To pedestrians and guests dining on the patio, the punch was truly devastating.

"That'll teach you to keep your hands to yourself, you piece of shit."

"Kyle, knock it off. He's harmless," Ally interceded.

"Ahhh," James groaned, holding his face. *Why doesn't she just say 'inconsequential'?* "Don't worry, I'm alright."

"I'm sorry, James," Ally said as she knelt down beside him. "Are you okay?"

"Ally, let's go!" Kyle fumed.

"Just get in the car. I'll be right there," Ally answered.

James sat up, dabbing his bloody nose with the back of his hand. He smiled at the view he had of Ally's breasts as she leaned over him.

"What is it?" she asked.

"Oh, nothing. Just this whole situation, I guess."

"Well, I apologize. He's obviously a bit protective."

"Do you love him?"

"What?" Ally said, caught off guard.

"Never mind. Don't answer that." Ally stood up as James struggled to his feet and dusted off his khakis. "Just make sure you don't ever love someone who doesn't love you back."

"Okay," Ally said, slightly confused by the course of the conversation.

"Do you promise?"

"Yeah, I promise."

"There's nothing more tragic than seeing a woman like you wasted on a man who doesn't love her. It's kind of like Poe's philosophy about the death of a beautiful woman."

"Oh, I see," Ally said, pretending to get the reference. "Well, I better go. Are you sure you don't need anything?"

"Yeah, I'll be fine. Tell Kyle it was nice to meet him."

"I will. Take care," she said, forcing a smile.

"Bye." James waved goodbye to Ally's thighs peeking out from her skirt, which involuntarily hiked up as she climbed into the bucket seat. *I'll miss you.* James could feel his cheek begin to swell and see it crowding the vision in his left eye.

The restaurant began to die down around 10:45pm. Soon after, Tony invited James to join him out back.

"Come on, James LaMotta. Have a seat in your corner. We'll get 'em in round two," Tony said, holding the door open for James with one hand, a bottle of liquor in the other.

"Yeah, yeah."

"Geez, you look like shit. Are you sure you didn't scare any customers? I should have had you in the back washing dishes tonight."

"Does it look that bad?" James asked as he sat down.

"Nah. It's not as bad as it was. You just look a little uglier than normal. That's all."

"Oh, thanks a lot, asshole."

"Hey, I'm just callin' it like I see it." Tony paused to light a cigarette. "You know you are allowed to punch back, or even duck."

"Yeah, it all happened so fast. I guess I didn't even think about it. Plus, I probably deserved it a little."

"Yeah, what's that all about? Oh, wait. I almost forgot," Tony said, realizing he had yet to offer James a drink. "Here you go."

"Thanks," James said, accepting the bottle of Pendleton Canadian Whiskey. "He was pissed because I kissed Ally."

"When?"

"Last Saturday."

"How did this happen?"

"I bumped into her downtown. She was being pretty damn flirtatious. There's really not that much to say. I kissed her, and she didn't like it."

"You mean, she acted like she didn't like it," Tony said with a grin.

"No, it was pretty clear. She wasn't too happy."

"Well, shit. At least now you can say you've been in a fight."

"Yeah," James laughed. "I'll put it on my résumé."

"Speaking of which, how did that interview in Seattle go?"

"Good, good. I'm supposed to hear from them by the end of next week."

"You feel like it went well though?"

"Yeah, I actually do."

"Well, let me know when you find out. If you're leaving us, we're gonna have to throw you a big ass going away party."

"I will. Don't worry."

"So, at least not everything's going to shit, huh?"

"Well, that's just the thing. I went over to this Amber girl's house last night. Did I ever tell you about Amber? I was sort-of dating her last year. Kind of a plain girl, but pretty cool."

"The name doesn't ring a bell, but I'm sure you told me about her at some point."

"Well, anyway, I go over to her house thinking that if I tell her I changed—See, I kind of pissed her off because I wasn't that into her for a while—Anyway, I tell her that I've been thinking a lot lately and—"

"Wait, you changed?" Tony asked in snarky way.

"Well, I thought I did," James said, taking the question literally.

"What does that mean?"

"I don't really know. I think that's sort of the point."

"So, what happened?"

"Well, first of all, there was another guy over there watching a movie."

"Ooh, that's not good."

"And, long story short, I told her what I had to say,

thinking she was still really into me, and, well, it sort-of blew up in my face."

"She got mad?"

"No. She just didn't respond the way I wanted. She said I was too late and then she just went inside."

"Shit, that's cold. Well, why don't you take another drink and pass it this way."

"Oh, I'm sorry. Here."

"Nah, take another drink first."

James complied. "So, yeah. Things haven't been all that great," he said, handing the bottle back to Tony.

"Well, at least she didn't become a lesbian."

"Touché."

"But I am sorry to hear about your string of bad luck."

"That's funny," James chuckled.

"How so?"

"Well, it's just that, I don't remember the good luck too well."

"That's why there's this," Tony said, passing the bottle to James.

"Thanks." James took a sip. "But seriously, how do you do it?"

"Do what?" Tony asked as he continued to lazily blow smoke into the air.

"Act like you don't care. You don't take things so seriously all the time."

"I don't?"

"Well, it doesn't seem like it. Not like the rest of us."

Tony took a long meditative drag from his cigarette and exhaled. "I guess I don't worry about all the stuff that can happen to me, like most people. You know, like the things we can't control."

"What can we control?"

"How we react."

"Do you believe in God?"

"Whoa, pass that back," Tony said, eagerly gesturing for the whiskey. "Why do people only ask those questions when things are going bad?"

"I don't know."

"Do you want someone to blame?"

"What do you mean?"

"I've come to think that people who believe in God, or fate, or whatever, do so partly because they want to be able to blame someone else when life gets fucked up. No offense."

"I don't know if that's it, but I just haven't seemed to get the results I want for, what seems like, most of my life."

"Well, if I can continue philosophizing..."

"Please."

"I think most people feel that way. I also think that everybody wants to critique the process too much," Tony said, beginning to speak elaborately with his hands. "They're constantly unhappy with the results, so they try to do something different in order to create the response they want. Religious people have to pray more. Fat people have to choose a new diet. Poor people have to find ways to make more money. Lonely people have to do something exceptional to get someone to like them. But, if you look at people, they all seem pretty fucking miserable; no matter what they do. When you really look at them, anyways."

"So, what do you suggest?"

"Well, what I do is, I don't try to constantly change

how I live. I ignore the process," Tony said. Making 'process' an imaginary box between his hands. "I focus on the results instead, or at least how I look at the results. See, I tell myself, 'You can't always get what you want, unless you change what you want.'"

"Huh?"

"People get frustrated by their hopes, their dreams, and their desires more than they get frustrated by what actually happens. I simply adjust my view of what's 'supposed to happen'."

"It sounds like you're lowering expectations."

"It might sound like that, but if I'm quote-unquote happier, who's to say?"

They both sat for a moment in silence, pondering the words hanging in the moonlit smoke.

"Wow! That's some pretty fucking good whiskey, huh?" James asked, breaking the serious mood.

"I'll drink to that."

Before Tony could finish taking a pull, Luis burst through the door. "Hey, there you guys are. We thought you'd left."

"Why would we do that?" Tony responded.

"I don't know. You've just been gone awhile."

"Sorry, we'll be right in. Come on, James. We'll finish this after work," Tony said, shaking the half empty bottle.

LIVES

Sunday

The West Valley Community Church auditorium was nothing more than rows of blue chairs assembled across the length of a basketball court. The chairs were laid down in an amphitheater style, enveloping the podium on its raised promontory. James sipped black coffee and wondered if people were staring at his bruised and swollen face. He had used moderate amounts of his mother's foundation to cover up unsightly pimples throughout high school, but James now owned nothing that could hide the brownish-purple smudge currently painted below his left eye.

One of the associate pastors had just called the names of five people who were going to share about 'how they have come to know Christ.' The first person in line was a track star at his high school. The second was a heavily tattooed thirty-something whose shaved head shined brightly in the lights. The third was a nine-year-old girl with colorful barrettes in her hair. The fourth was a twenty-two-year-old mother of three. And the fifth was an eighteen-year-old refugee from the Republic of the Sudan. All of them were beaming with varying mixtures of caffeine and God's love.

"Hi, my name's Jason, and God has really made a big difference in my life lately. I noticed this spring that most everyone on my track team was really nasty to each other. People bickered and constantly talked behind each other's back, and sadly, I wasn't much different. But then I started praying about the issue every week in Bible study..."

James zoned out while Jason finished his story. Instead, he studied the audience members, still wary of his own appearance. James was eventually startled back to attentiveness as the audience applauded Jason for his testimony. *How are you supposed to clap with coffee in your hand?*

Then, Darren took center stage and spoke into the microphone with a gravelly voice.

"Hi, my name is Darren, and I've been clean and sober now for eighteen months because of the immense change God has created in my life. I left my parent's house when I was seventeen: lonely, confused, and most of all, angry. I began to sell and use drugs. I resorted to sleeping on people's couches, and, in effect, was homeless throughout most of my twenties..."

Again, James's attention wavered, having felt like he'd heard that miracle before. *I've still got to figure out what I'm gonna tell Janet tomorrow.* His concentration was soon broken by the applause given for Darren.

For some strange reason, as Ashley, the little nine-year-old, made her way across the stage, James was already interested in what she had to say. Maybe it was her blonde hair held neatly in place by several pink and purple barrettes. Maybe it was her white Sunday dress. Maybe it was the black buckled shoes she still wore with socks. Whatever it was, James was entranced.

"Hi, my name is Ashley, and I asked Jesus into my heart..."

As Ashley uttered those last few syllables, James felt a rush of air escape from within his chest, followed by a slight quiver of his lip.

"...I felt so much better after I did it because I knew I was going to live with him forever in heaven..."

Suddenly, James felt tears coming. He tried exhaling deep breaths through his mouth, but he couldn't hold back the tears. He began to cry. *I can't believe I'm crying. I can't remember the last time I—*

"...And the other thing I learned in Sunday school is that Jesus loves everyone in the whole world. I think everyone should know what it's like to love Jesus."

As the congregation enthusiastically clapped, James doubled over, unable to control his now audible sobbing. He set his coffee down and buried his face in his hands. People sitting near him turned in their chairs to identify the noise's source, mildly perturbed by the disturbance. However, one of his neighbors was more comforting as they lightly patted him on the back saying, "There, there."

James heard nothing from the other two volunteers. His head filled with its own noise: the guttural whining, the clearing of snot, the heaving chest. His forehead was so tense it began to ache. The whole time thinking to himself, *Why is this happening?*

As one last applause was given, along with a collective 'amen', the head pastor, pastor Goodell, stepped on stage and spoke into the mic.

"If anyone here today wants to take that step and accept Jesus Christ as their personal Lord and Savior, there will be members of our prayer team in the back waiting to guide you through that process at the end of our service today. Please, feel welcome to join us."

Before the pastor could begin his sermon on Psalm 44, James wiped his face with the sleeve of his shirt and side-shuffled past the members of his row on the way to the bathroom, empty coffee cup in hand.

James sat inside a stall for several minutes trying to compose himself. After finding relative comfort in the fact that he was completely alone, James gave in and allowed himself to cry freely. Wails echoed off the metal framing of the stall.

*   *   *

One day, when James was six, his mother asked him what he'd learned that morning in Sunday school.

"I learned that God sent His Son to die for our sins," James answered from the front seat of their 1988 Nissan Skyline, before a parent was chastised for such negligence.

"Very good. And why did He do it?" his mother asked.

"Because He loves us?"

"Yes, that's right. You're so smart!"

James didn't respond. Instead, he examined the picture he had colored. It was one of those classic Sunday school coloring pages with an emblematic scene depicted on one side and fill-in-the-blank questions about that day's scripture on the other.

"Whatcha think'n about?" James's mother asked after a few minute's pause.

"Nothin' much."

"It doesn't look like it. It looks like your head is full of ideas."

"Well, I did think of something."

"What is it, honey?"

"God is Jesus's dad, right?"

"Yeah, basically."

"Well, did God love Jesus?"

"Yes, very much so."

"Then why did He let Him die?"

"Wow, that's a good question!" his mother said, thinking carefully of the best way to answer. "You see, it's all part of His plan. He sent Jesus to Earth to show us how to be good people; then, when the time came, Jesus sacrificed Himself so He could live with His dad again in heaven, forever."

"Is my dad in heaven?"

"No, honey. He's here on Earth too. He just lives very far away."

"Do I need a dad to get to heaven?"

"No, James, of course you don't."

"Why not?"

"Because God loves you like you're His own child. Plus, I love you extra because your father's not around."

"Hmm," James pondered. "I guess that makes sense."

"I hope so. A lot of grownups have trouble with this stuff too."

"Really?"

"Yeah."

James scrutinized the passing scenery for a few moments.

"Mom?"

"Yes, honey?"

"Was it part of God's plan for my dad to live far away?" James asked as they stopped at a red light.

"Ooh, can I take a look at your picture?" she said, pointing towards James's lap. "Oh my gosh, it's beautiful! Look, you even stayed inside the lines!"

* * *

Once his reservoir of tears had been exhausted, James dried his face with wads of toilet paper. *I feel like the poor girl at prom whose date is out dancing with someone else.* He then spun off clumps of extra toilet paper and shoved it into his pockets before walking out to take a look at himself in the mirror. *Man, Costa was right. I do look like shit.*

After reentering the auditorium, James didn't bother returning to his seat. He decided to throw his coffee cup away instead of refilling it and simply stood in the back, trying to listen intently to the last bit of the pastor's message.

"...And, so it seems, to know God is to know pain, much in the same way that in order to be truly thankful one must know what it is like to go without. We do not learn of love or joy or peace or harmony through their constant presence; instead, we learn most about these things in their absence. And there is our lesson. God allows us to experience depths of great anguish in order to fully appreciate the vastness of his unending love; and, in that way, He lets us experience the difference between life with Him and life without Him. In other words: heaven and hell.

Let me leave you with the words from Matthew 8:26,

right after the disciples ask Jesus to save them from the storm. 'He said to them, "Why are you afraid, you men of little faith?" Then He got up and rebuked the winds and the sea, and it became perfectly calm.'

Please bow your heads with me."

James closed his eyes during prayer for the first time in many years.

Most of the congregation had left by the time James approached pastor Goodell, who had exchanged hearty handshakes and wide smiles with many of those exiting the auditorium.

"Hey, it's nice to meet you."

"It's nice to meet you too. And your name is?" pastor Goodell asked as they shook hands.

"James."

"Well, it's nice to meet you, James," pastor Goodell said to finalize the greeting.

"I was actually wondering if we could talk sometime."

"Oh. Well, what about?" pastor Goodell answered as he examined James's reddened eyes and bruised face.

"Uh, kind of about the 'being saved' stuff."

"Well, I could set you up with one of our prayer team members who'd be happy to talk with you now."

"No, I've already done that. You know, when I was little. I was hoping we could talk, just the two of us, sometime this week, if that's alright."

"Sure," pastor Goodell said, sensing a peculiar desperation in James that he had gotten used to over the years, but still acutely recognized. "Here's what I'll have you do. Call the church's main office tomorrow and ask to schedule an appointment with me. My secretary will set it up. I'm afraid she knows my schedule much better than I do," he said with a self-deprecating grin.

"Okay, I'll call tomorrow," James said, straight-faced.

"It was a pleasure to meet you, James," pastor Goodell said, extending his hand once again.

"Yeah, you too. Thanks," James replied.

It was 10:55am when James walked through the church doors and out to his car. The sun was bright, and he had to shield his eyes as he thought about his upcoming decision. *Brian or Tori, huh? This should be easy...But I've thought that about a lot of things.*

Monday

"Can you explain a little bit about what influenced you to choose Brian?" Janet asked from behind her desk.

"Well, it wasn't an easy decision, but I tried to make it a simple one," James answered. "I disregarded everything I knew, or thought I knew, about either person and tried to evaluate each one as if I was looking at them for the first time."

"So, why Brian?"

"He's simply a better, more mature writer."

"And that's all there is to it?"

"Yeah. I figure if he's being considered for a writing position, that's about all it should come down to. Why? Do you need something more to tell them?" James asked, sensing there was a catch somewhere.

"No, I guess not. I just expected you to pick Tori for some reason."

"Why?"

"I don't know. I just thought you liked her more than Brian."

"I thought I was supposed to be acting professionally here," James laughed. "Plus, you and I should both be a little suspicious of the things I apparently like."

"Oh, yeah? Do you like working for me?"

"Now that's a trick question."

"Alright, alright," Janet said, getting the conversation back on track. "Do you, by any chance, want to be in here when I break the news to the two of them?"

"God, no. Not unless I have to. I've got plenty of work to do on my piece for this week anyway."

"Okay. I'll see you around lunch to go over that then."

"Sounds good."

"Thanks again, James," Janet said as she stood to shake hands. "I think you made the right decision."

"I'm hopin' so."

As James sat down at his desk, Janet signaled for Brian and Tori to meet in her office. Out of respect, James forced himself to watch as they passed, each one clearly uncomfortable with the situation. Brian walked by without making eye contact, while Tori threw James a cold, expressionless glance. *She's gonna get the wrong idea.*

After several minutes, the door to Janet's office opened again. James turned to notice that Brian was the first one through the door. The accelerated cadence of his clumsy steps proved his excitement. He walked over to James's desk.

"Hey, James; I just wanted to thank you," Brian said, extending his hand.

"Don't thank me, Brian. It makes me feel like I did you a favor. And that's not what I did."

"Well, either way, I appreciate it," his hand still hanging there.

"Okay," James conceded, as he dispassionately

squeezed Brian's stubby, little hand. "I'll talk to you later, Brian."

"Okay."

Brian seated himself at his desk as Tori emerged from Janet's office, probably just having been notified of her last day of employment. She walked proudly, with shoulders back and chin up, but avoided all eye contact as she retreated straight to her desk. Tori stood in her cubicle, rummaging among things for a few moments, until she suddenly threw her bag over one shoulder and hurried out the back door. James jumped up to follow her, but only got as far as the exit. He watched through the glass doors as Tori climbed into her car. He could have easily opened the door and called to her but decided to let her go. *I think I kinda know how she feels.*

Tuesday

James pulled into *Idyll's* parking lot at 8:48am. He walked past a short row of cars and noticed Tori sitting on her usual curb, smoking an early morning cigarette. She had dyed her hair a chocolate brown, surprisingly void of any bizarre streaks or highlights.

"You're here early," James said.

"I was waiting for someone," Tori answered without making eye contact.

"You were waiting for me?"

"I'm gonna tell Janet," she said, ignoring the question.

"Tell her what?"

"Don't play dumb."

"I'm not playing dumb. What the hell are you talking about?"

"I'm gonna tell her you slept with me," Tori said, looking up at James over her right shoulder.

"What?" *Are we in high school?*

"Yeah. I'm gonna tell her that you promised me the fulltime job if I slept with you. We'll see how that works out for you."

James hurried closer to shrink the distance her voice had to travel. "Are you fucking crazy?"

"Maybe," Tori said, batting her eyes as she looked up at him.

"What good would that do? It'd make you look as bad as it made me."

"I don't know about that." She began to speak in a childish voice. "I'm just a poor young girl who is so easily manipulated by the men in her life, especially those in charge of making such important decisions," Tori concluded with the pouty lips of a spoiled five-year-old before she took another drag.

Wait, she obviously thinks that I knew I was making the decision the whole time. James circled around her other side and sat down next to her. "I still don't understand what you think you'll get out of this," James said calmly.

"Well, they'll obviously have to have someone else make the decision. So, maybe there's a chance I'll get it this time. Plus, it'll be fun to see you squirm a little."

"I hate to burst your bubble, but Janet would just end up making the decision herself, and she wanted to go with Brian the whole time. The only reason she asked me to make the decision was because she thought it would look bad if she chose Brian outright. In fact, she was surprised that I didn't choose you yesterday. She thought I favored you for some reason."

"You're full of shit."

"I wish." James paused as Tori studied him with a look of concern. "So, I don't think it will look too good if someone who is having sex with fellow employees, you, tries to discredit her biggest supporter, me, in order to get a job she has no chance of getting."

"Well, even if I didn't get the job, it would still fuck

you over. Or does Janet encourage you to fuck interns?"

"That's just it. If you really want to fuck me over, why are you telling me all this? Usually, people's diabolical schemes don't involve warning their potential victims."

"Well, I thought—" she cut herself off to take another drag as Rob, the local news writer, pulled into the parking lot. They both waited for him to gather his things and head into the building.

"Go on," James said to Tori after exchanging salutational gestures with Rob.

"I want you to go clear it up with Janet, so I don't have to. Tell her you changed your mind. Make up something about Brian if you have to."

"You know what I think?" James asked with a lighthearted grin.

"What?"

"I think you kinda like me." Tori looked at him with disgust as she blew smoke from the side of her mouth. "Yeah, I think you're doin' all this to get my attention. You think I might do something for you because of the other night."

"Whatever."

"Either that, or you're pissed because your plan to get the job didn't work out."

"You're an asshole! You knew exactly why we hooked up and then you turned around and gave the job to that fat little shit, Brian, who I know you don't even like, because you wanted it to mean something when we fucked when you should have known better."

"Ah, but there's something you should know," James said in an attempt to diffuse the situation.

"What?"

"I had no idea that I was choosing between you and Brian the night we slept together."

"What are you talking about? Of course you did."

"No, I didn't. Janet told me I was making the decision right before I left for Seattle. That would have been—last Wednesday."

"You're lying."

"No, I'm not. When we met up, I was completely oblivious. And that's what I'm trying to tell you. If you go tell Janet about us, it's going to make you look really stupid because she knows she told me that I was making the decision way after she told you two."

"Are you serious?"

"Yes."

"You swear?"

"I shouldn't have to, but yeah. Think about it. If I thought that us getting together was some weird work-related thing, I wouldn't have been all bent out of shape the next morning when you weren't around. Plus, who uses sex to get a job that pays $25,000 a year? This isn't Hollywood."

Tori hugged her knees and stared straight ahead.

"I have an idea though," James said after a brief silence. "If I get this job in Seattle, which I think is pretty likely, then I can suggest you to be my replacement here."

"Why would you do that?" Tori mumbled with her chin tucked into her legs.

"To be nice, I guess. I might think you're a little crazy, but that doesn't mean I want bad things to happen to you. I didn't pick Brian to get back at you."

"Why did you pick him?"

"Quite frankly, he's a little more stable. You're a good

writer, but just a tad unpredictable," James said, emphasizing the small space between his finger and thumb. "I tried pretending I was the boss, and I think most bosses would have come to the same conclusion."

"Do you really think you'll get the job in Seattle?"

"Yeah, I'm pretty confident. Lauren's recommendation has to go a long way. And they'd be silly not to consider you to replace me here. They know your work. They wouldn't have to interview a bunch of people. It just makes sense."

"There's only one problem."

"What's that?"

"I kind of already sent an email to Janet."

"What do you mean?"

"I already sent her an email explaining what you did—what we did."

"When?"

"Last night."

"Why the fuck did you do that?"

"I was a little messed up last night—"

"Drunk?"

"That too. I—I just figured that you wouldn't cooperate, and I'd have to do something drastic. I guess I thought it was the ace up my sleeve."

"That sounds incredibly stupid. You do realize that, even if I would have done what you asked, you'd still have the same problem, right?"

"We."

"Sorry, we'd have the same problem."

"Yeah, I'm starting to realize it wasn't the greatest plan. I was just a little frantic after finding out that someone had chosen Brian over me," Tori said with an admonishing look.

"A little frantic? Fuck! What time is it? Is Janet here yet?"

"It's 9:06, and yes, Janet's here already."

"Fucking shit!"

"Why are you so worried? I thought you said that Janet would know I was lying. About you offering me the job, not the fucking part, of course," Tori said through a twisted smile as she stood and looked down at James.

"I knew Janet would know you're full of shit, but that doesn't mean I want her to hear it."

"That's right. She could tell Lauren, and he could tell that guy in Seattle and..." Tori mused with a fake sincerity.

James shook his head scornfully.

"Don't worry. I'll take care of the Janet situation as long as you do something for me."

"How will you do that?"

"I don't know. I'll make something up. I'll tell her I was so mad about not getting the job that I made up this ridiculous lie in order to get back at you. Don't worry, I'll tell her you're innocent."

"Good—"

"As long as you do something for me."

"What?"

"You said you'd suggest me to be your replacement if you got the job in Seattle, right?"

"Yeah."

"Well, I want you to put it in writing. So I know you'll come through on your promise."

"Okay."

"And, I want you to write me another

recommendation in case you don't get the job and I end up having to look for work."

"Fine."

"There's just one more thing."

"What?"

"On the second recommendation, you have to pretend to be my boss; because if this doesn't go over smoothly, Janet may not end up being the best reference in the world."

"So, you want me to lie?"

"Basically. Or I could just go home and let you try to explain that email to Janet."

"Okay. I'll do you this one favor."

"Oh, you'll be doing yourself a favor, James. Trust me."

"Trust you? Now that's funny."

"Oh yeah?"

"Yeah. But let's get inside. I've got some actual work to do and you've got some talk'n to do," James said as he stood up. "Oh, I almost forgot. Is that your natural hair color?" he asked as they began moving towards the door.

"Almost."

"Well, I like it."

"Thanks. What happened to your eye?"

"I got punched, actually."

"Wow, does it hurt?"

"Not really. As long as I can see out of it, I'm fine."

Wednesday

James showed up at West Valley Community Church at 1:55pm for the appointment he scheduled earlier in the week.

"Hi, I'm here to see pastor Goodell," James said as he approached the desk of the first secretary found within the church office doors.

"And your name was?"

"James."

"Okay, hold on one second, please," she said as she picked up the phone and pressed a single button. "Hey, Cathy, there is a James here to see pastor Goodell. Does he have a two o'clock appointment? Uh huh. Yeah, of course," she said, then hung up the phone. "That was pastor Goodell's personal secretary. If you'll just have a seat right there, he'll be out in just a minute."

"Thank you."

"You're welcome."

James couldn't remember being anywhere inside a church besides the sanctuary or a Sunday School classroom. It felt strange to see the inner workings, the administrative details of which the average churchgoer was unaware. James scrupulously looked for a man pulling levers behind a curtain somewhere, but no such wizard was found.

A few minutes later, pastor Goodell opened a door to James's left.

"Hello, James, come on back."

After shaking hands, pastor Goodell led James down a quiet, relatively bare hallway. The walls were a heavily textured white, and each door frame was painted a dark brown. Once they got to his office, pastor Goodell motioned towards two leather chairs positioned on either side of the window.

"Go ahead and take a seat over there."

"Alright, thanks," James said as he sat down. "Wow, you sure have a lot of books."

"Yeah, I've collected quite a few over the years." Shelves, almost ceiling high, completely covered two of the four walls.

"Have you read them all?"

"I don't know if I've gotten to every single one, but most of them, yeah."

"That's got to feel good, though."

"What do you mean?"

"Oh, just possessing all that knowledge. I imagine it must be comforting to feel like you fully understand a subject."

"Well, I don't pretend to fully understand anything, but it does feel good to have tried so fervently. Besides, having lots of knowledge doesn't always measure up to having the right kind of knowledge. Some find comfort in that."

"I can see that," James nodded in affirmation.

"Now, James, you don't regularly attend this church,

do you?"

"No, sir—"

"Please, call me Paul."

"Okay, Paul. And no, I don't come here very much. I kind of go to a different church every week."

"So, you do regularly attend church, just not this one?"

"Correct."

"And why is that?"

"I'm not sure if I know. I tell myself certain things that I know aren't true. I guess the biggest thing is that I've never wanted to become part of a congregation, to have people know me and expect things of me. It would make me feel dishonest."

"Why dishonest?"

"Because I've never felt that I was there for the same reasons as everyone else."

"So, why do you come to church?"

"I don't know. It feels like sort-of an instinct, or a kneejerk reaction to something. I'm usually a very analytical person, but this is something I haven't thought that much about. It's just something that I do."

"Interesting. And is this what brought you here today? This uncertainty?"

"No, not really—I mean, there's probably some connection—but I had something more specific in mind."

"Okay, so why don't you tell me a little bit about that? And we'll see if there's a clear connection or not."

"Alright. Well, I was particularly moved by the testimonies from this week's service. Or, at least, a few of them."

"Hmm, go on."

"And I guess the easiest way of saying it is - I felt sort of jealous."

"How so?"

"Well, they seemed so happy. So sure of the process. Especially that little girl."

"What do you mean when you say 'process'?"

"The whole asking-Jesus-into-your-heart thing."

"If I remember correctly, on Sunday you didn't want to meet with a member of our prayer team to help you with that."

"Right. I grew up going to church, so I've already done it before. Or, at least, tried to. And that's really my question, or my problem, I guess."

"Please explain."

"At one point in my life, but not any time recently, I was sincere about wanting to be a Christian, or Godly, or whatever you want to say."

"Okay."

"And part of why I've drifted away from it for the last ten years or so is because I never felt any different. I never felt a change."

"I think I understand."

"Yeah, and that's why it hit me so hard to see those people talking on stage. They genuinely looked and sounded like they had a life changing experience, and I have no ability to relate to what they were saying. What am I missing?"

"First of all, James, I can assure you that you aren't missing anything. There isn't anything wrong with you. God simply works differently in each of our lives. Our job is to make ourselves available to God and allow Him to work through us, even if we aren't sure of His plans."

"But doesn't it say things in the Bible about once you're filled with the Spirit you'll be consumed by joy and peace and all that other stuff?"

"In a sense, yes, but James, God does not, in any way, promise to rid your life of troubles once you've become a believer. Quite the contrary—"

"I get that, and that's not what I'm saying exactly. I'm wondering why when I tried to do what all those people on stage did, I didn't feel any different. I know it's not supposed to be some magic spell that instantly transforms everything you see and feel, but I have never really felt any different, at any point in my life. It makes me feel like I've been lied to. It makes me feel like God's not listening."

"I can't attest to your feelings exactly, but I surely can't deny them either. What I do know is that God does reward those with pure intentions. It may not be immediate, and it may not be in the manner that we foresaw, but He accepts all who truly seek Him and are able to put Him before all other things."

"So, what are you saying?"

"Is it possible that you had a misunderstanding of what you were trying to do when you were younger?

"I guess so. Contemplating the eternal destination of your soul when you're a seven or eight-year-old does seem pretty weighty. But I can specifically remember being in high school and recognizing the gravity of what I was doing."

"What was your motivation for becoming, or remaining, a Christian at that time?"

"In high school?"

"Yes."

"I guess I felt that it was the right thing to do. That's what my mom had taught me. That's what people at church had always said. I just felt kind of confused and alone, and I wanted that to go away."

"Did you notice that you didn't mention God in your answer?"

"Uh—no."

"I can't accurately speak of the past, but perhaps, full commitment and devotion to God was not part of your pleas for salvation. And I don't want this to sound harsh, but maybe you had ulterior motives when you prayed to God."

"Are you saying I didn't do it right? That seems rather absurd."

"I can't see into your heart. Only you and God can do that. But the James sitting in front of me seems very conflicted and resentful, so, in that way, the James of the past doesn't really matter anymore. Let me ask you this: do you want God in your life now?"

"Not really," James said after a small hesitation.

"Then why are you here?"

"Because I want to know how I'm supposed to believe in something that doesn't seem real to me."

"Honestly, I don't know if I can help you with that. In some people's minds, faith is an inherently irrational act, and I can't necessarily give reasons for you to believe if you don't first want to believe."

"So, what should I do?"

"Put yourself in a position to openly and willingly listen to God, as if for the first time."

"Sorry, but God doesn't talk to me."

"He talks to you through His Word."

"Oh, okay. And once I've done that?"

"Talk to Him."

"And what if he still doesn't listen?"

"I believe He will."

Thursday

Thursday morning staff meetings always felt dull to James, but especially now because he figured he only had a few more to attend. The tone of these meetings was always the same. Lauren reflected on the product that just went out the day before, and then he identified areas where he thought the paper could improve. These comments were always very global in nature, never directed at any specific individuals. It was more of a weekly revisiting of *Idyll's* mission statement, if anything else.

Most of the staff had assembled themselves around the long oval conference table when Tori arrived. James looked up to see her stroll into the room wearing a black, cropped, Moto jacket pulled tight over a gray graphic tee. She circled around James's side of the table, towards the empty seat on his left.

"Can I sit here?" Tori asked, moving into the seat before James could even answer.

"Sure." As Tori sat, James noticed the short plaid skirt that completed her outfit. *Ooh, I love those.*

Since Tuesday, everything seemed to work out fine concerning Tori's threats of impropriety. Soon after their discussion, James saw Tori go into Janet's office, and when she came out, neither woman seemed troubled in any way by what had transpired. James was relieved to not have to deal with Tori's time bomb, but his curiosity begged to know what was said behind those doors. Either way, both he and Tori seemed to stand in good graces with Janet as the week progressed. It was to be Tori's last.

Lauren was sitting down to begin the meeting when James leaned over and whispered to Tori.

"I'm surprised you're even here. If they had told me it was my last week, they couldn't tie me to that chair."

"O ye of little faith. If you get that job like you're supposed to, it won't be my last."

"I see." *Since when does she quote the Bible?*

As Lauren spoke from the head of the table, James intermittently snuck glances at Tori's thighs. *I can't help it; they're in my natural line of sight.* Tori's thin stalks of flesh were pale and relatively undefined, yet the way she delicately draped one over the other was enough to command James's attention.

After Lauren stressed the importance of illuminating the smaller populations of Arbor Valley worth celebrating, the meeting broke and scattered everyone to their respective working areas. James's efforts to brainstorm for his next story were somewhat thwarted by his growing anxiety about the job for *Northwest Metropolitan*. He hadn't suddenly become less confident, he merely acknowledged that the week was coming to a close and that his life, at least professionally, was hopefully about to encounter great change.

At 10:26am, James got up and went to the men's room. He stopped to examine himself in the mirror for a few moments until Tori sprang through the door.

"What the hell are you doing in here?" James asked, backing away from the mirror to avoid appearing vain.

Tori temporarily ignored the question as she dead bolted the door behind her and then stooped down to see if there were legs visible inside the two stalls. She had apparently shed her jacket in favor of the gray off-the-shoulder tee, adorned with a black, screen-printed skull. "I haven't been able to properly thank you," she said, as she stood up and moved towards James.

"Did anyone see you come in here?" James asked, still stepping back.

"I don't think so," Tori said, still moving forward.

"I do like that skirt."

"I figured you would," Tori said as she grabbed him by the shirt and kissed him. James's arms hung lifelessly at his sides. Still holding his shirt, Tori backed James into one of the stalls. With a light shove, James stumbled back onto the toilet.

"Here?"

"Why not?" Tori stepped into the stall, maneuvered the door behind her and fastened it shut.

"But I—"

"Don't worry. I've got this under control." She crossed her arms, grabbing the hem of her shirt, and pulled it over her head to reveal a black, strapless bra. "Trust me. Remember?" Tori said as she flung her shirt over the top edge of the stall. "Now," she inched closer, reaching out for his hand, "touch me here." She took his hand in hers and placed it between her legs.

"Oh, wow," James muttered involuntarily.

"You see? I didn't bother wearing any panties today. I

didn't want to make things complicated." Her voice was now a soft whisper.

Only she could say that with a straight face.

"Now kiss me, here," Tori said, inviting James to kiss her neck.

"Like this? James said as he consented.

"Oh, yeah. Just like that," Tori said, her hands moving to the back of James's head and neck.

Is this really happening? His free hand ran up the back of her skirt.

"Now, I want you to fuck me," she said, grabbing a hold of his belt.

Wait! "Wait!" Her words rang in his ear. "Hold on," James said, letting his hands drop.

"What? What's wrong?" Tori pulled back to look at him. "I won't tell anybody."

"It's not that. I just—don't think I want to do this."

"Why not?" Tori asked, withdrawing.

"I don't know. It just doesn't feel right."

"So, all of a sudden you're some morally superior being?"

"No, that's not it. I'm just not sure anything good will come of it."

"Listen to you. Are fucking serious?" Tori asked as she grabbed her shirt and turned to unlatch the stall door.

"Sorry. I don't mean to embarrass you."

"I'm not embarrassed. You're just a fucking idiot, James," she said, pulling her shirt back over her head. She then took a brief glimpse in the mirror before hurrying out. "Oh, by the way," she said over her shoulder, "there never was an email. Thanks for the references though." And with that, she unlocked the door and left.

James waited for a moment in case anyone saw Tori leaving the men's room.

I think I made a wise decision.

The middle hours of James's work day consisted mostly of futile internet searches and watching the cursor blink teasingly on a word document that was predominately bare. James was thankful to be interrupted by a call on his cell phone at 2:05pm.

"Hello?"

"Hi, this is Stacy calling from *Northwest Metropolitan*; may I speak with a James Dall?"

"This is he."

"Hello, James. I regret to inform you that we've decided to go in a different direction in regards to the position you interviewed for last week," Stacy said, seemingly from a script."

"Wait, what? Are you serious?"

"We want to thank you for your time and wish you luck in your future endeavors."

"Wait, can you tell me why?"

"I'm sorry, James. That information is not available to me at this time."

"Well, can I just talk to Jack—I mean, Mr. Wheaton for a second?"

"I'm sorry. I'm afraid he's busy at the moment."

"Oh, my god." James's forehead sunk into his left hand. "Can you at least tell me what he's like?"

"Excuse me?"

"The new guy. Whoever they hired."

"Uh—" She gathered her words. "All I can say is that he is very qualified and that it was not an easy decision."

"That's it?"

"I'm sorry. I have other business I need to attend to. Is there anything else I can help you with today?"

"No. I guess not."

"Well, good luck to you in the future. Goodbye."

"Bye." *Good Luck? What's that?*

James was home by 3:00pm, unable to stomach any more tedious work for the day. When he passed by Tori's desk, her eyes remained fixed on her computer screen. James noticed that she was once again wearing her jacket and that her legs were carefully concealed under her desk. James didn't bother telling Janet that he was leaving.

On his way home, James stopped by the liquor store, and for no apparent or particular reason, he asked the store clerk to help him pick out something new, something he'd never tried before. After a barrage of suggestions that James rejected, having tried them all already, he settled on a bottle of Courvoisier VS cognac. "Now it's going to taste a little sweet, which is something you'll have to get used to, but I really think you'll like it in the end," the clerk said.

"Well, it sounds good, it looks good, I'm bettin' it tastes good too," James said.

"Yeah, you'll see."

James poured himself a drink and called Cade right after setting his work things down on the kitchen table. He reached Cade's voicemail and left a listless message that equated to 'call me back'. *He must be teaching summer school.*

James took sips of Courvoisier to pass the time and

soon found himself examining the internet history on his laptop. *It's the same shit over and over again.* After growing tired of that somewhat introspective activity, James checked his email and found no new messages from anyone or anything for which he genuinely cared. He finished his first drink and got up to make another. *This is good. Very floral. It's different.*

After recapping the bottle, James chose to ignore the computer, bypass the recliner, and make himself comfortable on the couch, with his back to the TV and his feet propped up on a cushion. His only view was of the kitchen, but James wasn't really looking. Instead, he held a deep, unfocused stare as he replayed many of life's recent events. His greatest comfort came from his powers of recollection and his drink's juxtaposition of temperature as it left the glass and entered his body. It was a soothing burn. A delicious toxin. An instigator and a loss of thought. *This is just what I need.*

At 4:16pm, James's phone rang. It was Cade.

"Hey, what's happenin'?" James said with a manufactured joviality.

"Nothing much. I just got your message," Cade returned.

"You doin' anything tonight?"

"Ah! You're killin' me with these weeknight invites."

"So, it's a 'no'?"

"Well, I can double check when I get home, but it's tough for us family guys. You know that."

"Yeah, I guess I should."

"What did you have in mind?"

"Oh, nothin'. Just—somethin'. You know the drill."

"I'm afraid I don't know that one anymore."

"Really? You're missin' out," James said sarcastically. "Well, while I have you on the phone, I should let you know that you don't have to help me move."

"Why? What happened?"

"I didn't get the job."

"The one in Seattle?"

"Yeah, that one."

"Shit, that sucks. When did you find out?"

"A few hours ago."

"Oh, I understand. Well, let me talk to the wife and I'll let you know what the deal is."

"Don't worry about it too much."

"No, I'll ask. But in case I'm not coming out tonight, please let me know if I can help you out in any way. I mean, who knows? Maybe you'll still want to move somewhere, right? You know, mix things up. You are almost thirty."

"Yeah, I'll let you know."

"Okay, I'll call you back in a bit."

"Alright. Later."

James got up and poured himself another drink while he scrolled through the other names in his phone. He paused on one, looked up for a moment and thought to himself: *Why not?* He then filled his glass up a little more than last time and made his way back to the couch as the phone began to ring. He plopped down, careful not to spill his drink, as he reached another voicemail greeting. *I might as well.*

"Hey, Amber, this is James. Call me back when you get this. I'd really like to talk to you."

James received no other calls that night. Cade texted back at 5:08pm to tell James that he wouldn't be able to hang out, but that was all.

Besides reclining and sipping Courvoisier, James spent segments of his evening fighting off boredom by examining all the things he owned. First, he looked in his bedroom closet, full of jeans and sweatshirts, a few collared shirts, and slacks. He stared at them. Then he held his glass of cognac up to his eye and tried to make out the shapes of the various objects through the golden-brown liquid. He said things to himself as he peered through the glass, like "Ah ha!" or "There you are." He then turned around and studied a small bookshelf, repeating the same process: first looking, then trying to see through the cognac. Then into the living room, where he knelt down to view his movie collection. Then the kitchen. And so on and so on.

When James concluded, he sat down and checked his phone. *Well, I guess that's it. That's all I've got.*

Friday

James started the day by telling Lauren Duvall he was quitting, citing 'a family emergency' as the reason.

"I obviously cannot comment on the seriousness of your family emergency, but are you absolutely positive that your absence needs to be a permanent one?" Lauren questioned.

"That's the one part I am certain about," James answered.

"At the risk of sounding insensitive: are you sure you can't postpone it awhile? You are leaving us in a difficult situation here."

"I realize that, and I'm sorry, but I'm afraid it's unavoidable at this point."

"Would you still be quitting the *Northwest Metropolitan* if you had gotten the job with them?"

"I don't know. I hadn't really thought about that. These last few days have been a bit of a blur. But I suppose I would have to."

"Well, it will be a shame to lose you." Lauren stood up to shake his hand, appearing gracious in defeat. "Stop by Janet's office, would you please? She'd like to have a word with you, I'm sure."

"I will. And thank you, Lauren, for this opportunity, and for trying to understand my situation. I appreciate it."

"You're welcome, James. Good luck."

James turned and walked the length of the office towards Janet's door, not expecting her to be so understanding.

After repeating the same rehearsed story about a family emergency, void of any specific details, and the fact that he would be moving, probably out of state, James once again apologized for the short notice.

"Shit! What do we do for the next couple of weeks, especially this one coming up? We just can't find someone off the street and throw them in the mix."

"Yeah, I know. I'm sorry about that. I wish there was something more I could do."

"Me too."

"What about Tori?"

"What about her?"

"She could take my spot. Or at least fill in for a while."

"Tori?" Janet chuckled. "We just rewarded Brian. Why would we let her leapfrog over him? Besides, I think your instincts were right about her. She hasn't even shown up today. It's as if she doesn't even care about getting a reference. She probably thinks she's so brilliant she doesn't need one."

Yeah, something like that. "Well, maybe give Brian my job and give Brian's to Tori. It's the only suggestion that came to mind. Sorry."

"Yeah, well, I guess it isn't your job to worry about it," Janet said as she appeared to drift off in thought.

"Well, I'll get out of your hair. Thanks for everything, Janet," James said as he stood and extended his hand.

"Good luck, James," Janet responded without any hint of recognition that this would probably be the last time they ever stood face to face.

James left and drove home at 9:47am to start packing up his things. *I think quitting one job is enough for now.*

James scrutinized each object or article of clothing before boxing it up. Keeping it only when he could tell himself: *I can see the value in this,* or *I need this.* This process caused the box labeled 'Goodwill' to fill up faster than any of the others. James didn't appear to find this disconcerting; instead, he motored around his small apartment with a calm efficiency, seemingly at peace with each decision.

After making 'significant progress', James made a few phone calls. He called his landlord to negotiate the retrieval of his deposit. He called Goodwill to look into donating most of his furniture. He called his cable and internet providers. And to reward himself for such adult endeavors, he poured himself a drink. It was 12:17pm.

Once he had properly scripted his upcoming conversation, amid sips of Courvoisier, James felt the need to pour another drink as he picked up his phone and called his mother.

"Hello?"

"Hi, mom."

"Oh, hi, James. Say, this is kind of an odd time to be calling. Is everything alright?"

"Yeah, everything's fine. Well, sort of."

"What's the matter? Did you get that job?"

"No. That's kind of why I'm calling."

"They're crazy. They don't know a good writer when

they see one."

"I don't think that's it. I think it's me."

"Wha—"

"I have a feeling I'm not the kind of person they want. And I'm beginning to agree with them."

"Listen to you. I didn't raise someone to think it was okay to tuck their tail between their legs."

"Maybe that's the problem."

"What problem?"

"I don't think I've been living in reality—or not aware of it at least. And it's because of some of the stuff you taught me—and some of the stuff I taught me, to be fair."

"And what did I do that was so horrible?"

"You didn't do anything horrible. I just don't think you gave me an accurate view of things."

"Such as?"

"God. My father—"

"Your father? What does he have to do with anything?"

"Everything, I'm afraid. I want to know where he lives."

"What? You know he hasn't tried to contact you in all these years."

"I don't care, mom."

"Well, maybe you should. I think it says something about a man when—"

"You're probably right, but can you just give me the contact info you have?"

"Fine! I just don't know what good this will do..." James' mom trailed off as she searched through some old drawers. "The last thing I have says he's living in Sacramento."

"Really? That's not very far at all."

"What'd you expect?"

"I don't know. I guess I always imagined he was on the other side of the world or something. At least that's how it always felt."

"James?"

"Yeah?"

"Why are you doing this?"

"Because I've been looking at things one way my whole life. It's time to try something different."

"And how is your father going to be of any help?"

James hesitated a moment, in contemplation. "I think he'll listen."

James sat down at his computer and bought a one-way plane ticket immediately following the conversation he had with his mother. After that, he sent a detailed email to Cade informing him that he would act as James's so called 'executor of estate', which really meant that Cade would inherit the responsibility of selling all of James's unwanted possessions not suitable for Goodwill, among other chores. James followed with a text, cognizant of a 'normal' person's work schedule, to ensure that Cade viewed the email in a timely manner.

At 4:17pm James drove to Un Monde Parfait. When he walked in, Tony was behind the bar.

"Hey, Jimmy Black Eye!"

"What's up, Costa?"

"What are you doing here? You're not on till six."

"I'm not working tonight."

"What are you talking about? The schedule says you're here from six to close. I even had a couple bottles set aside for—"

"I'm quitting."

"You're what? What are you talking about?"

"I need to talk to Dan. He's here, right?"

"Is this about a girl?"

"No. I'm moving to Sacramento."

"Sacramento? I thought it was Seattle."

"Yeah, that fell through. This is different."

"Different how?"

"It just is. I'll tell you later. Can you take a quick break after I get done talkin' to Dan?"

"Probably."

"Okay. I'll see you in a bit," James said as he started walking towards the back of the restaurant.

"Hey, James."

"What?" James said, turning over his shoulder.

"I heard Ally broke up with her boyfriend," Tony said with a furtive smile.

"Oh, yeah?" James asked, turning all the way around.

"You should make a move. Now's your time. She's working the floor right now."

James squinted for a moment as he pondered. *Don't turn to look. Don't turn to look.* "Nah, I've done enough," he said as a grin was forming.

"Alright, suit yourself."

"I'll be back."

"Okay. No worries."

As James knocked on Dan's office door, he heard a muffled "come in" that prompted him to enter.

"Hey, James, what can I do for you?"

"Well, to be frank, I've had a family emergency come

up and I'm moving to Sacramento tomorrow."

"Moving! Really? What happened?"

"Well, it's kind of personal, but I'm going to be with my father." James had rehearsed responses such as these.

"Well, shoot, I'm sorry. Is it serious?"

"In a way, yes."

Dan leaned back in his chair and interlaced his fingers behind his head. "So, you're quitting, is that right?"

"I'm afraid so."

"Shit. I guess we'll have to move the schedule around a little bit," Dan said almost to himself while looking into the opposite corner. "Did you tell Tony yet?" Dan asked after a moment of contemplation.

"Yeah, just now."

"Well, do you have your employee ID card on you?"

"Yeah, I do," James said as he pulled out his wallet.

"Well, I hope everything goes alright. With your family and all, I mean."

"Thanks," James said, handing over the ID card. "Is that it?"

"Yeah, I guess so. I mean, you were a good employee, but we'll manage; don't worry."

"Well, thanks for—being understanding," James said, forcing out the last few words.

"Yeah, no problem. You take care, James."

"Alright." James nodded and left the office.

"How did it go?" Tony asked as James took a seat at the bar.

"Fine, I guess. He didn't seem too troubled by it."

"What'd you expect?"

"Well, my bosses at the paper—that's right, I've quit

twice today—actually tried to convince me to stay."

"Ah, that's just Dan being Dan. Plus, you weren't that great of a waiter anyway."

"Hey, thanks."

"What? I'm not here to bullshit you. Don't let your pride take a hit when someone reacts appropriately. I thought you learned that by now."

"I'm gett'n there."

"Here," Tony paused to pour a small glass of Buffalo Trace bourbon. "Have a drink."

"Am I paying for this?"

Tony just pointed to his nose, as if playing charades, and stepped away to help a customer. James sipped his drink slowly. *Don't turn to look. Don't turn to look.*

After James finished his drink, Tony said, "Let's go," and motioned him with his hand. As they stepped through the back doors, James asked Tony, "Isn't Dan still here?"

"Yeah. Why? You afraid he's gonna fire you?"

"No. I just don't want to get you in trouble, that's all."

"Don't worry. I'm on break. I'll be fine. Besides, check this out." Tony reached for two bottles he had stashed behind some crates. "This one's yours."

"Wow, 18-year-old Macallan. I'm impressed."

"Call it a going-away present."

"Are you sure?" James asked before breaking the seal.

"Yeah, I figure if I'm not stealing from the company a little bit, then I'm not taking full advantage of my situation. The way I see it, this is part of my salary."

"You're not on salary."

"You know what I mean."

"What if Dan comes out?"

"He won't."

"Well, cheers." They clanked bottles and then each took a pull.

"So, why you movin' to Sacramento?"

"I've been tellin' everybody it's a family emergency."

"But that's not true?"

"No. But in a way, it kinda is—at least for me."

"How so?"

"I just need a change, Costa. I've been livin' my life the same way for so long, and it just doesn't seem to be gettin' me anywhere. You know what I mean?"

"Yeah, I guess so. But why do you have to move to do that?"

"I'm not really sure, but I kinda want to force myself to see everything for the first time. You know, start from scratch."

"Hmm. But why Sacramento?"

James took a long sip. "That's where my father lives."

"Oh! That makes sense."

"Does it?"

"I just mean—you never met him, did you?"

"Not really. He left when I was like two. I mean, I think I remember him, but I can't really tell if those are my memories or memories I've made up after lookin' at pictures and stuff." James paused for another sip. "It's weird how that happens, huh?"

"Yeah, if it wasn't for camera phones, I wouldn't remember any weekend from the past half decade." Tony raised his bottle in honor of his own wit.

"True," James said with a chuckle. "But seriously, our memory is so subjective. The things we think we know become our biggest obstacles." He noticed Tony smiling. "What?"

"I'm just glad to see that your present is working. You just opened the bottle and you're already a philosopher."

"It tends to have that effect, huh?" James said, holding up the bottle and peering through it in Tony's direction.

"It does. That's why I'll miss times like this."

"Me too, Costa. That's one thing I do know."

James was packing up a few remaining boxes when he heard someone knock at the door. *What the*—It was 8:23pm. James opened the door to find Amber clutching a bottle of red wine.

"Can I come in?"

"Of course."

"I wanted to say goodbye."

"How'd you know I was leaving?"

"Cade and Tara told me."

"Did they tell you to come here?"

"No."

"Good. I like the thought of it being your idea."

Amber smiled. "I brought you this," she said, finally offering the bottle as a gift.

"Oh, thanks." James turned the bottle in his hands. "Cabernet, huh?"

"Yeah, sorry about that. I know it's not really your drink, but to be honest, I wanted to get something I like, in case you weren't here. Now I feel bad," Amber said as her hands searched for a place to rest comfortably.

"Don't. If you like it, then it's worth a shot. Plus, I think my tastes are expanding a bit. Or at least they should." James looked up from the bottle and at Amber. Her lips parted in a smile and then she looked down at her hands. "Should I pour us some?"

"I think I'm okay for now."

"Alright. I'll just set it over here." James placed the bottle on the counter. "You want to sit down?"

"Sure."

"Sorry about all the boxes," James said as Amber sat down on the couch and he sat on the recliner, opposite her.

"Do you need any help?"

"I think I've got it. Why? Does it look like I need help?"

"No, not really. I just thought you might need a woman's touch. You know? To stay organized."

"I have always liked a woman's touch," James said. Amber laughed out of politeness. "I'm sorry. That was cheesy."

"That's alright. For some reason, I always liked your dumb jokes."

"What about my good ones?"

"What good ones?"

"Ouch! I guess I walked into that one."

"So, are you taking all of your stuff with you?"

"No. I'm actually trying to bring as little with me as possible."

"What are you going to do with it all?"

"Cade's gonna help me sell some of it. And I'll probably donate the rest."

"Wow. I know they're just things, but don't you kinda feel like you're selling off little pieces of yourself?"

James nodded.

"I've always felt creepy about the idea of my things being in the hands of strangers." Amber shuddered at the thought.

"Yeah, that's kinda the point."

"What? To feel creepy?"

"No, the 'selling pieces of yourself' part."

"Hmm. You know, for a rash decision, you seem to have thought about this quite a bit."

"I don't know if 'thought' is the right word."

"Oh yeah? Then what?"

"I don't know—'revelation'?"

"Have you still been going to church?"

"Yeah, but it's not like that. It's sort of an intuitive deal. You know when something just makes sense? Things become clear—and in focus."

"What's become so clear that showing up at people's doorsteps in the middle of the night and moving to California makes sense?"

"I don't know exactly. I just know it's not this." James spread his arms in reference to the contents of his apartment. Amber responded with a slow, contemplative nod, her bottom lip protruding a bit.

"Do you want me to tell you why I called?"

"Yeah." Amber shrugged and pressed her palms together, then wedged them between her knees. "If you want to."

James paused for a moment. *How should I say this?* "I want you to come with me."

"What!?"

"Yeah," James said with a nod of reassurance.

"You can't be serious." Amber blushed and looked about the room.

"I am."

"But—that doesn't make any sense."

"That's exactly why I'm asking."

"This whole thing—it doesn't sound like you."

"I know," James said with an eager grin.

Amber got up to pace the length of the room. "Why? Why are you asking me this?"

"Because you're about the only good thing in a life I'm about to leave behind."

"I thought you weren't taking anything with you."

"I said 'as little as possible', and I wasn't talking about you, I was talking about all this stuff."

"Where did all this come from?"

"You know, I'm not completely sure, but somehow, I find that oddly comforting."

"Well, I think that makes one of us."

"I know I don't deserve it, but I know I can be good to you, and that's something you deserve."

Amber shifted her gaze to the window and said nothing.

"Should I open the bottle of wine now?" James asked, to break the silence.

"Sure," Amber said, still looking out the window.

James walked to the kitchen, looked through a few cupboards, found what he was looking for, and then promptly opened the bottle. "I hope you're not above drinking wine from a mason jar. That's all I have." James started to pour before waiting for an answer.

"That's fine," Amber said as she walked towards the kitchen.

"Here you are," James said, setting half a jar of wine on the counter.

"James, you know I can't go with you to Sacramento, right?"

"I know it's asking a lot, but I thought it was still important to say to you."

"Well, thank you." Amber reached for her wine. "And thank you."

"Cheers," James said, holding up his wine carefully, for it was almost full. "To missed opportunities."

"To knowing the truth," Amber reciprocated.

They each took a drink.

"Oh, there's one more thing," James said, striding over to a stack of boxes.

"What is it?"

"It's my writing journal," he said, offering it to her. "I want you to have it. You know, a little piece of myself."

"Won't you miss it?"

"We'll have to see."

Saturday

The plane began boarding at 8:25am. James paid extra for his ticket so he could board early and claim a window seat. In the past, he had always chosen the aisle, preferring easy access to the bathroom over the scenic view. But today, James figured he could tolerate the forty minute flight, once you factor in the hour gained, even after an abundance of coffee and a mini bottle of Wild Turkey, because today was different. Not yet in any discernible way, but in the fact that it was the first day that was not going to be like all the others.

While the plane filled, James recited his normal preflight prayer to himself: *Hot girls, no fatties. Hot girls, no fatties. Hot girls, no fatties.* The aisle seat was quickly taken by a woman in her early fifties who displayed no specific peculiarities. James continued his silent incantation.

Eventually, a young man with glasses conservatively dressed in khakis and a quarter-zip sweater claimed the middle seat. James said nothing. He only secured his seat belt and watched the ground crew busying themselves outside until they pushed back from the gate.

Once in the air, James became enamored by the

vastness of the surrounding mountain ranges. *From the valley they look so two-dimensional; being up here makes them feel so endless.* Although nearly paralyzed in appreciation, James still had the courtesy and the awareness of others to tilt his chair back and move his head as to allow his row-mates to see. James glanced at the man next to him and noticed that his vision was fixed forward on some religious text, although James couldn't determine which one. The woman in the aisle seat was fast asleep. James turned back to the window until drink service arrived.

The woman awoke just long enough to utter, "Ginger ale, please." The man in the middle ordered coffee, and James asked for orange juice. Once the beverages arrived, James reached into his backpack and retrieved another mini bottle of Wild Turkey. James looked at his watch before unscrewing the cap. It was 9:27am. *Eh, it's almost 10:00.* James proceeded to modify his drink, which went seemingly unnoticed by his neighbors, and thus, made James even more comfortable.

As he sipped, James curiously peered at the man's book through the corners of his eyes, still unable to determine what it was. The man felt James looking over his shoulder and turned to prevent an awkward silence. "You can borrow it when I'm finished, if you'd like."

"Oh, sorry." James waved his free hand apologetically. "I guess I was just curious."

"That's okay. I figured it was a decent excuse to introduce myself. My name's Mark," he said extending his hand. "But I'm serious about you borrowing the book."

"I'm James, and that's okay. I should have minded my own business."

"Like I said, it's quite alright."

"So, what's it about?" James asked after a brief pause.

"It's about planting churches."

"Oh," James responded blankly.

"Yeah, I actually just finished up a two week long trip visiting newly developed churches, trying to learn what went well and what struggles they've encountered." Mark's face lit up with enthusiasm.

"So, are you a pastor? You look pretty young."

"Yeah, I get that a lot. I'm actually twenty-nine, and I'm the youth pastor at a church in Arden-Arcade."

"Are you planning to start your own church then?" James asked between sips.

"Lord willing. Provided that I find some place I feel called to and that will be a good fit for my wife and kids."

"How many kids do you have?"

"Three. Two girls and a boy."

"Wow."

"Does that seem like a lot?"

"No, not really. It's just that we're the same age—and our lives seem—pretty different."

"Different can be good."

"Yeah, I guess so."

"Well, do you want a family? Is that something you wish for in the future?"

"I don't know, maybe." James took another sip.

"I hope you don't mind my asking, but do you go to church?"

"Uh, not really."

"Not really?"

"Well, I've gone to church quite frequently in the past, but I'm not really there when I'm there. If that makes sense."

"Like, you don't want to be there?"

"Not exactly. I choose to go; no one's forcing me. I just don't get much out of the experience."

"But you keep going?"

James took a sip as if it was a deep breath. "It's kinda like going to the doctor. You show up expecting to get healed, and you end up spending most of your time in the waiting room thumbing through magazines no one cares about. When you finally get to see the doctor, he tells you a bunch of stuff you already knew, he takes your money, and then you're free to go. When you leave you aren't any healthier, but you make another appointment because you feel faintly satisfied that you did something you were supposed to."

"Wow. That's a pretty impassioned analogy."

"Thanks. It must be the orange juice," James said with a grin.

"Do you mind if I jot that down?"

"Not at all." *I'm usually the one trying to quote people.* "I don't mean to be offensive, by the way. My perspective on things has been changing lately, and I think I've yet to process it all."

"That's okay. You're just being honest," Mark said as he made notes on the inside cover of his book. "I actually find those observations helpful. Lots of people have trouble finding a church that's right for them."

"Yeah."

"That's part of what this book's about. All the ideology and daring involved with starting something new meeting up with the practical logistics of—how would you say—spiritual market research."

"Hm."

"Are you from Sacramento?"

"No, I'm moving there right now actually."

"Really? Well, I'd like for you to come check out Trinity United and give us a try."

"We'll see. Thanks for the invite though."

"Let me give you a card," Mark said, searching his pocket.

"Okay." *Even pastor's have cards?*

"That way, if you ever have a question about anything, you can just give me a call. Okay?"

"Sounds good. Thanks."

And as quickly as the conversation started, it concluded just as abruptly. Mark recorded a few more notes and then turned to smile at James, but he was already looking out the window appreciating the now Nevada desert. James slurped his last bit of orange juice and whiskey, leaving only the stained ice cubes to melt within the plastic cup. Mark reopened his book and resumed reading, while the woman in the aisle seat continued sleeping.

James walked through the jetway and into the terminal. *Where's the city?* James reached into his pocket for his phone. *It looks like we landed in some farmer's pasture.* It was 9:32am Pacific Time. Mark's card also came up in James' grasp, so he studied it for a moment. *What are the odds?*

Strangely, James was not apprehensive about talking to his father for essentially the first time in his life. He simply dialed the number his mother had given him and tossed Mark's card in a trashcan as he passed.

"Hello?"

"Hi, is this—Jerry?"

"It is."

"This is James. I'm here in Sacramento."

"James who?"

"James Dall."

"You're kidding. James James?" Jerry's voice fluttered slightly with a mix of confusion and excitement.

"Like, your son, James."

"Holy shit!"

"Yeah, something like that."

"Well, what are you doing in Sacramento?"

"I'm movin' here."

"Wow! When?

"Uh—now, I guess."

"Do you need a place to stay? Or do you wanna at least get together or something? I mean, if you feel comfortable."

"Yeah, I was hopin' to."

"Wow, James. I can't believe it. Man, it's good to hear your voice." Jerry laughed a kind of laugh that hid the evident emotion behind it.

"It's good to hear you too."

"Look, I'm sorry I never—"

"Don't. That's not necessary," James said as he came to a stop.

"Are you sure?"

"That's not why I came."

"Well, why did you come? If you don't mind my asking."

"To be honest, I haven't quite figured that out yet, but I think the fact that I am here is more important than why."

"Okay." Jerry paused. "Well, do you need a ride from the airport?"

"If you don't mind, that'd be great."

"Sure. Just let me gather myself here and I'll leave as soon as I can. I'm assuming this is your number?"

"Yep."

"It might take me a bit to get out there, but I'll call as soon as I pull up."

"Alright, that sounds good."

"Okay, well, I'll see you in a bit."

"Okay, bye."

James put his phone back in his pocket and then checked his watch. He then proceeded to take his watch off and set it to Pacific Time. *Now let's see if we can find our way from here.* When James's eyes racked their focus, he realized he was standing in front of a stretch of carpet that was also a brilliant piece of installation art: a series of digital photographs woven together to provide an aerial view of the Sacramento River and its surrounding landscape. *Yeah, this is it.*

ABOUT ATMOSPHERE PRESS

Atmosphere Press is an independent, full-service publisher for excellent books in all genres and for all audiences. Learn more about what we do at atmospherepress.com.

We encourage you to check out some of Atmosphere's latest releases, which are available at Amazon.com and via order from your local bookstore:

Relatively Painless, stories by Dylan Brody
Nate's New Age, a novel by Michael Hanson
The Size of the Moon, a novel by E.J. Michaels
The Red Castle, a novel by Noah Verhoeff
American Genes, a novel by Kirby Nielsen
Newer Testaments, a novel by Philip Brunetti
All Things in Time, a novel by Sue Buyer
Hobson's Mischief, a novel by Caitlin Decatur
The Black-Marketer's Daughter, a novel by Suman Mallick
The Farthing Quest, a novel by Casey Bruce
This Side of Babylon, a novel by James Stoia
Within the Gray, a novel by Jenna Ashlyn
Where No Man Pursueth, a novel by Micheal E. Jimerson
Here's Waldo, a novel by Nick Olson
Tales of Little Egypt, a historical novel by James Gilbert
For a Better Life, a novel by Julia Reid Galosy
The Hidden Life, a novel by Robert Castle
Big Beasts, a novel by Patrick Scott
Alvarado, a novel by John W. Horton III
Nothing to Get Nostalgic About, a novel by Eddie Brophy

ABOUT THE AUTHOR

Matt Edwards was born and raised in Boise, Idaho, formerly the Northwest's best kept secret, where he developed an affinity for literature: both the challenge of understanding it and the potential to be understood through it. This propelled Matt to study English at Boise State University and devote himself to teaching high school English in the Boise area since 2006. Matt now enjoys sharing his life of passions with his wife and their one and only son. In his free time, if Matt's not training for marathons, he's writing fiction and poetry, mostly about gods and fathers and good, strong drinks. *Ways and Truths and Lives* is his first novel.